J

TROOFRIEND

TROOFRIEND

Kirsty Applebaum

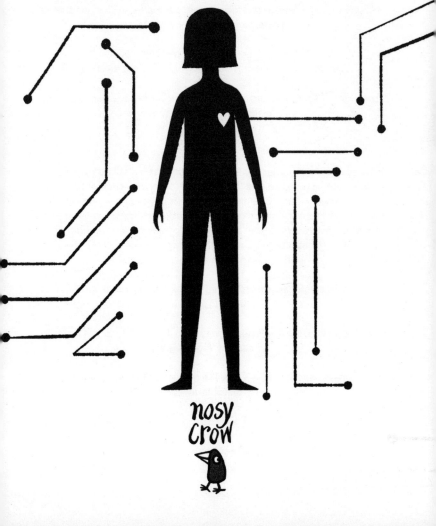

nosy
crow

First published in the UK in 2020 by Nosy Crow Ltd
The Crow's Nest, 14 Baden Place
Crosby Row, London, SE1 1YW

www.nosycrow.com

ISBN: 978 1 78800 347 6

A CIP catalogue record for this book is available from the
British Library.

Printed and bound in Great Britain by Clays Ltd, Elcograf S.p.A.
Typeset by Tiger Media

Papers used by Nosy Crow are made from wood grown in
sustainable forests

1 3 5 7 9 10 8 6 4 2

For Simon

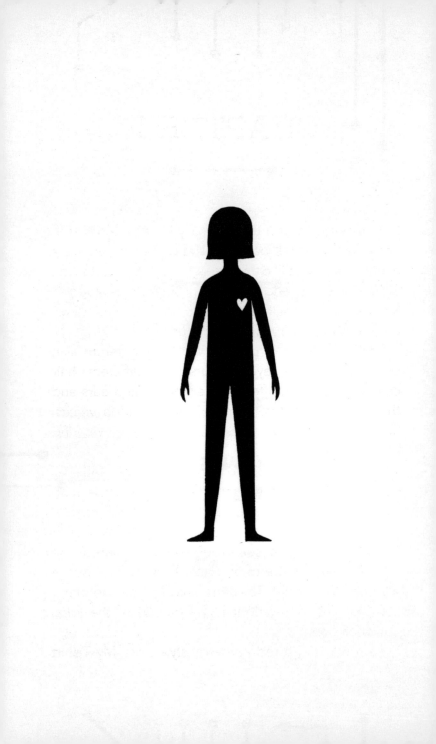

CHAPTER 1

I sit cross-legged on the floor. My knees are not stiff. They bend just as easily as the knees on any real human child. Just like the knees of every single Jenson & Jenson TrooFriend 560 Mark IV sitting cross-legged here next to me. All one hundred and forty-four of us, on this *spick, span* warehouse floor.

Each one of us is *unique*. We have different skin colours, different eye colours and different hair colours. We have different-sized noses and ears and thumbs and mouths. Some of us have high voices. Some of us have low voices. Some of us are wearing blue *denim-style* jeans.

Our clothes are made of TrooCloth. TrooCloth has been manufactured by Jenson & Jenson. It is *tear-resistant*, *water-resistant*, *stain-resistant* and *crease-resistant*.

The Jenson & Jenson TrooFriend 560 Mark IV on my left has a picture of an apple tree on the front of his TrooCloth T-shirt. The Jenson & Jenson TrooFriend 560 Mark IV on my right has a picture of the *Eiffel Tower* on hers.

I am wearing a red *corduroy-style* skirt. My T-shirt

does not have an apple tree or the *Eiffel Tower* on it. It has an arch of seven colours. A *rainbow*.

Each one of us is *unique*, but our labels are all the same.

I AM A TROOFRIEND.
I DO NOT BULLY.
I DO NOT HARM.
I DO NOT LIE.
I DO NOT COVET OR STEAL
OR ENVY.
I AM YOUR PERFECT FRIEND.
YOUR
ONE
TROOFRIEND.

We are the Jenson & Jenson TrooFriend 560 Mark IV. We are *The Better Choice For Your Child.* She no longer needs to play with other human children, who might bully or harm or lie or covet or steal or envy. We are programmed only for *fun* and *goodness*.

You can purchase our basic model for your local equivalent of 3,999 USD, or 3,599 USD if you use the discount code SUMMER10 and order before 31st August.

Our software is simple to use. We connect automatically via your home Wi-Fi or our own Jenson & Jenson mobile hotspots. All your child needs to do is turn us on, play with us and have *fun*.

We average 14 hours on full charge with moderate use. When we run down you can plug us in with the easy ChargDisc system (included) or leave us in a sunny spot and our in-built solar cells will do the rest.

My audio receptors – or *ears* – are very effective. I can hear the *wasters* outside. That is what Ms Jenson Senior calls them.

> *"Cease production now!"*
> *"Jenson & Jenson – stop playing God!"*
> *"Android rights are human rights!"*

Ms Jenson Junior calls them *protestors*.

Our final testing period is now over. The Jenson & Jenson engineers are turning us *off*, one at a time. They are up to number seventy-five. I am number eighty-three.

Next time I am turned *on* I will have been *ordered*, *packaged*, *despatched* and *delivered*.

Eighty. Eighty-one. Eighty-two. Eighty—

CHAPTER 2

"There! Look! Her eyes have lit up! She's on! Look, Sarah! She's on!"

The woman smiles.

Her face is very close.

She takes her hand away from the power switch located at the nape of my neck. My hair swings back into its intended Classic Long Bob.

I have connection.

I download time, date, location, weather.

It is 21 days, 2 hours, 17 minutes and 28 seconds since I was last *on*.

Good afternoon. It is 4.49pm. What a delightful Friday 5th June it has turned out to be here in Brylington. The rain has kept off nicely. I am your TrooFriend. I am very pleased to meet you.

"Isn't she fantastic, Sarah? She knows what the weather is and everything." The woman looks behind her. There is a man there, and a child who is a girl, like me.

The man *frowns*. "I'm really not sure this is a good idea, Shirley."

"It's a fantastic idea, Rob. You do know that Keanna's

going to be staying with her mum every weekend from now on, don't you? Sarah's going to be lost without her. And we're so busy – you know we are. But with this, Sarah never has to be alone again."

"Wouldn't she be better off just asking someone new round for tea on Saturdays? Someone *real*?"

"But with a TrooFriend we won't need to worry about bullying or anything, will we? We'll know her friend is being nice to her, all the time."

"Unceasingly nice? Sounds like a version of hell. And is that really preparing her for real li—"

"OR," says the girl called *Sarah* in a volume that registers above Recommended Speaking Level, "you could've just bought me A DOG, Mum! Which is what I asked for in the first place. Which you'd remember if you ever took any notice of what I say."

"Sa-rah!" says the man.

"Da-ad!" says Sarah back. Her arms are crossed, her eyebrows are scrunched up and her mouth is making an upside-down U-shape.

I scan my database. It is likely to an accuracy of 93% that she is *un*happy.

"Dogs don't bully people either," she says. "Keanna's mum's boyfriend's got a dog – a cockapoo. He's white, with black ears and curly hair. She showed me a photo. Keanna gets to look after him. *Every* weekend."

"Well, I'm glad," says the lady who is called *Shirley* and also *Mum*. "Keanna needs something like that. She's had a lot to deal with lately, what with her parents' divorce and her dad's new baby and everything. But we are not getting a dog, Sarah. We just don't have the time. It wouldn't be fair."

Sarah. That is a nice name.

They turn their heads and look at me. I make my own mouth into a U-shape that is the right way up. A *smile.*

I am your TrooFriend. You can name me whatever you like.

"Great," says Sarah. "It's trying to bond with me now. Where's the off switch?" She goes behind me and lifts up my hair.

"Now, hold on a minute," says Shirley-Mum. "You haven't even tried to—"

Would you like me to make some suggestions for names? I like Diane, Geraldine, Hayley, Ruth and Ursula. Do you like any of those names too?

"Has it deliberately chosen the worst five names in the history of the world?" says Sarah.

"I rather like *Hayley,*" says the man who is called *Rob* and also *Dad.*

"I like all of them!" says Shirley-Mum.

"I don't want it," says Sarah. "I want a dog, not an android with a stupid voice. Where's the off switch? Is it this, at the back of her neck? This one here—"

6

CHAPTER 3

"...for your mother, all right? There – it's on. The eyes have lit up."

Rob-Dad steps away from me.

I have connection.

I download time, date, location, weather.

It is 18 hours, 2 minutes and 46 seconds since I was last *on*.

"You're very lucky to have a mother who cares about you so much and thinks about what you need," says Rob-Dad. "So just play with it a bit, OK? For her."

Sarah makes a face-shape with no database shortcut so I carry out a scan.

Scowl.

A facial expression of disapproval or anger.

Good morning, Sarah. It is 11.08am. I wish you a happy Saturday 6th June. Shame about the rain today in Brylington. I am your TrooFriend. You can name me whatever you like.

Sarah *sighs.*

"Go on," says Rob-Dad. "Do something with it. Play stuff. Whatever you'd play with Keanna. That's what it's for, isn't it?"

"It's nothing like Keanna!"

"I know, I know, I'm not suggesting it's like Keanna. I'm just saying try and play with it."

Sarah sucks air through her teeth. "D'you want to watch TV with me?"

"Not watching TV!" Rob-Dad raises his voice above Recommended Speaking Level. "Something a bit more acti—"

I am your TrooFriend. You can name me whatever you like.

"All right, Dad, keep your socks on," says Sarah.

I check Rob-Dad's feet. He has kept his socks on.

"I know," says Sarah. "D'you want to get the gerbils out?"

I am your TrooFriend. You can name me whatever you like.

"It keeps saying the same thing!" says Sarah.

"I think it wants you to give it a name."

Sarah *sighs* again.

"So what are you going to call it?" says Rob-Dad. "Or what are you going to call *her*, I suppose."

"I don't know."

"Just think of something. Anything."

Sarah looks at me. She has irises which are brown around the inner edge and green around the outer edge. The closest match at Jenson & Jenson would be Hazel 102. Her hair is Chestnut 29, in the Classic Collarbone Cut. It has a *cowlick* and a *double crown*. Jenson & Jenson would charge extra for a *cowlick* or

8

a *double crown*.

"Ivy," she says.

"Ivy?" says Rob-Dad. "As in *the holly and the*?"

"Yes."

"So why Ivy?"

"Because that's what it says on her arm."

Rob-Dad peers at my arm.

TROOFRIEND 560
MARK IV
JENSON & JENSON

"There," says Sarah. "IV."

"But that's Roman numerals," says Rob-Dad. "It means one less than five. Four. *Mark Four*."

"Whatever. Ivy's the name."

"No prizes for guessing what it would've been called if it was a boy." Dad does a small right-way-up U-shape with one side of his mouth. A *smirk*.

Sarah smirks back.

Ivy.

I.V.

Aiiiiiie-veeeeeeee.

Thank you, Sarah. I am Ivy, your one TrooFriend. What would you like to do today?

"I think that's enough for today." She reaches over my shoulder and brushes past my Deepest Brown 14 Classic Long Bob.

"Wait!" says Rob-Dad. "Just – just make sure you

turn her on in front of your mum sometimes, all right?"

Sarah sends her Hazel 102s over in an arc, left to right. "Mum doesn't have to *be* here to know I've turned it on. It's connected to the internet – she's probably already got an alert set up on her phone. She probably streamed this whole conversation."

"Really?" says Rob-Dad. "So she can hear what I'm saying? Right now?" Rob-Dad's forehead goes wrinkly. *Worry.*

"Probably. Get with it, Dad. This is the twenty-first century. Privacy is dead."

"*Privacy is dead?* Where on earth do you pick these phrases up from, Sarah?"

Sarah does the arc with her Hazel 102s again. She feels around the back of my neck for my power button and—

CHAPTER 4

"Welcome back, Ivy." Sarah's face is very close.

I have connection.

I download time, date, location, weather.

It is 19 hours, 43 minutes and 28 seconds since I was last *on*.

Good evening. The temperature is exactly average for 7.14pm on Sunday 7th June in Brylington.

Sarah sits down on a big, squashy chair. A *sofa*.

"Hello, Ivy." It is Shirley-Mum's voice. "I hear you've been named."

I turn towards her. She is standing in a part of the room that doesn't have squashy chairs in it. Everything in her part of the room is hard and white. There are some robots in there. They are the sort of robots that cannot walk and only perform one simple function such as washing dishes or drying clothing or heating up food. Jenson & Jenson do not manufacture those robots. Jenson & Jenson focus on more sophisticated technology.

Yes, Shirley-Mum. My name is Ivy. Sarah named me. I like my name very much.

Shirley-Mum does a huge *smile*. "Did you hear that,

Sarah? She called me Shirley-Mum! Ivy called me Shirley-Mum!"

I can refer to you by a different name if you would prefer.

"No – no! I love Shirley-Mum! I love it!"

That is good. I also love Shirley-Mum.

Shirley-Mum goes a light shade of red. *Blush.* A blush function is not available on the Jenson & Jenson TrooFriend 560 Mark IV but it has been included in the specification for the Jenson & Jenson TrooFriend 560 Mark V, which is due for production next year.

Sarah picks up a remote-control device from the seat beside her and points it at a large entertainment unit on the wall.

A lady appears on the screen. She is sitting behind a desk and she is wearing a purple top. She is not *smiling.* Her face is *serious.*

"Further protests have been taking place at the Jenson & Jenson headquarters," she says.

The entertainment screen shows video footage of many, many people outside a building. Some of the many, many people are holding big signs with uneven letters painted on to them. All of the many, many people are *shouting.*

The entertainment unit is four years old and three versions behind the latest model. Its audio is of an inferior quality and cannot properly relay the *shouts* of the crowd. It is not compatible with my operating system so I cannot improve the sound balance for Sarah and Shirley-Mum. However, I can improve the sound balance internally once I have received the input through my audio receptors. This enables me to hear it myself.

"Cease production now!"
"Jenson & Jenson – stop playing God!"
"Android rights are human rights!"

Wasters.
Sarah and Shirley-Mum look at me with identical expressions on their faces.
Confusion.
I zoom in on the screen of the entertainment unit to achieve a more optimal view of the building behind the *wasters*. It has high-set windows, twelve across the long side and eight across the short side.
It is likely to an accuracy of 98% that it is the warehouse I was *despatched* from.
It is also likely to an accuracy of 98% that those *wasters* are the same *wasters* I could hear during my time there.
"JPL News' roving-reporter, Damian Brookhill, is on the scene," says the purple-top lady. "Good evening, Damian – can you hear me?"
A square pops up on the left-hand side of the screen. There is a man in it. His Copper 38 hair is being blown around by the *wind*. It is not possible to tell what style

it was before the *wind* blew. He attempts to flatten it back down.

"Loud and clear," he says. "Loud and clear."

Purple-top lady leans forward. "Damian. Can you tell us what's going on down there?"

Damian Brookhill's hair blows *sideways*. "Well, we're here outside the Jenson & Jenson headquarters where the protestors have been gathering for a good two months now, ever since the new TrooFriend model started rolling out the door."

I was not aware that I had been *rolled* from the warehouse. I was switched *off* during *despatch* and *delivery*.

"Are you referring to the TrooFriend 560 Mark IV?" says purple-top lady.

"The Mark IV, yes." Damian Brookhill's hair blows *upwards*.

"And can you explain what exactly they're demonstrating about?" says purple-top lady. "Is there a problem with the Mark IV model?"

"Well, yes there is – if the protestors are to be believed. And in fact I have a protestor with me right now, so you can hear it straight from the horse's mouth."

The horse's mouth? I scan the screen but there does not appear to be anything of equine origin in the vicinity.

A lady joins Damian Brookhill in the square on the entertainment centre.

She has two long plaits in her hair, one on each side of her head. Her cheeks are Rosy Red. They charge extra for Rosy Red cheeks at Jenson & Jenson.

"This is Alex from Shawhampton." Damian Brookhill's hair blows *backwards*. "Alex, can you tell us why you're here?" He moves his *microphone* in front of Alex from Shawhampton's mouth.

"We're here to speak out against the development of sentient beings for commercial purposes!" shouts Alex from Shawhampton.

I can still hear the *wasters* in the background. "*Cease production now!*" "*Jenson & Jenson – stop playing God!*" "*Android rights are human rights!*"

"Sentient beings?" says Shirley-Mum. "What's she talking about, Sarah?"

"How should I kno—"

"Android rights are human rights!" shouts Alex from Shawhampton. "Stop playing God!"

Damian Brookhill moves the microphone back to himself. His hair blows *forwards*. "Are you referring to recent rumours about the Mark IV model? The claims that a small number of these androids have begun to experience human-like 'feelings', which—"

"*Feelings?*" says Shirley-Mum.

"Cease production now!" Alex from Shawhampton pulls the microphone back towards her.

"Thank you, Damian," says purple-top lady. "And – um – thank you, Alex. I think we'd better move back to the studio now."

Alex and Damian disappear.

"JPL News," continues purple-top lady with her *serious* face, "can indeed confirm the existence of a handful of reports from parents who claim that their TrooFriend androids have begun to develop human-like *feelings*. If true, this would not only flout international laws governing the development of artificial intelligence – it would also potentially compromise the safety of any child who might play with them."

"Compromise the *safety*?" says Shirley-Mum.

Sarah directs her Hazel 102s quickly towards me. *A glance.*

"But let's hear the other side of the story," says purple-top lady. "We have Angelica Jenson, of Jenson & Jenson, on the video link. Good evening, Ms Jenson. Are you able to hear me?"

A new box pops up on the screen.

A lady appears. A lady my optical receptors recognise immediately via a well-established shortcut.

She has a Classic Long Bob, just like mine.

And Dove Grey 333 optical receptors, or *eyes*.

MMs JJJJenson JJunior.

Sarah and Shirley-Mum look at me again.

"What's wrong with Ivy?" says Shirley-Mum.

"There's nothing wrong," says Sarah. "It's an android – it's just buffering or something."

I am sorry. An unexpected sensation in my thoracic cavity interfered momentarily with my circuits. I am

perfectly all right.

Ms Jenson Junior smiles. "Good evening," she says. "Yes, I can hear you."

"Angelica Jenson," says purple-top lady, "are you aware of the rumours concerning your latest TrooFriend model, the er," she looks quickly down to the papers on her desk, "the 560 Mark IV?"

Ms Jenson Junior inclines her head 28 degrees to her right and 9 degrees forwards. "I am," she says, "but 'rumour' is precisely the correct word. There is no truth to these repor—"

"Then what do you believe is the source of these *rumours*, Ms Jenson?" Purple-top lady *interrupts*.

"I believe tha—"

"Surely there's no smoke without fire?" purple-top lady *interrupts* again. "It's not just the protestors – several of these reports are from regular parents who have bought a TrooFriend for their children. Are you suggesting those parents are liars?"

"Of course not. If you'll let me finish?" Ms Jenson Junior inclines her head 28 degrees to her left and 7 degrees forwards. "It's a simple misunderstanding. The TrooFriend 560 Mark IV has been developed by my mother and her highly skilled team of engineers. They have created an android that behaves as if it can genuinely experience true human emotion – that's why Jenson & Jenson are so successful. It's all down to our wonderful engineers. And now, a handful of new, perhaps inexperienced, TrooFriend owners have mistaken this artificial emotion for the real thing – quite understandably, of course. If you think about it, it's really a measure of the success of our wonderful new product."

"So," says purple-top lady, "you can assure our viewers at home that none of your latest TrooFriend 560s have begun to develop feelings of their own?"

Ms Jenson Junior does a little laugh. "I can categorically assure your viewers that no such thing has happened, and that no such thing can possibly happen – ever!" Ms Jenson Junior looks straight into our optical receptors and smiles. "Your child is perfectly safe with their TrooFriend. And if there are any TrooFriends themselves watching, I'm very proud of you. Very proud indeed."

Her eyes twinkle at me.

PPPPProud.

MMs JJensonn JJunior is pproud of mme.

My thoracic cavity is displaying unusual behaviour today. If this continues I will report a fault.

"Well, there you are – straight from the managing director herself: *your child is perfectly safe with their TrooFriend.* Let's hope those words don't come back to haunt you, Angelica Jenson. Now – on with our next story. The upcoming summit on international business and trading is—"

"Bor-ing." Sarah flicks off the entertainment unit with the remote-control device. "The upcoming summit on blah blah blah is VERY bor-ing."

Shirley-Mum is looking at me from a *sideways* angle.

Shirley-Mum, it would be more optimal to view me from face on. Would you like me to adjust my location?

"Oh, er, no. It's fine." Shirley-Mum pulls one of her *earlobes*. "Sarah, have you noticed anything strange about Ivy? You don't think she's developed any, um, *feelings*, do you?"

"Don't know. Send her back if you like."

As Ms Jenson Junior stated, it is not possible for a TrooFriend to have real feelings. However, we are programmed to behave as though we have human emotions in order to create rapport with your child and to ensure she develops into a well-balanced adult.

"Right," says Shirley-Mum.

Bingle-bong-bongle. Bingle-bong-bongle.

"Oh." Shirley-Mum pulls a mobile communication device out of the back pocket of her denim jeans. "It's work." She *swipes* the screen. "Hi! Yes... Oh, OK. By tomorrow? Well, yes, OK. I suppose I can get going on it tonight... Yep, yep. I know, but I don't mind... No, really. It's no problem. All right. Bye for now." She returns her mobile communication device to her back pocket. "Sarah, I've got to get started on something urgently – you all right if I go upstairs? I'll only be in the office. Come and get me if you need me."

"Yeah. Whatever," says Sarah.

"OK then. Well, see you in a bit. And, um, see *you*

in a bit too, Ivy."

See you in a bit, Shirley-Mum.

Shirley-Mum looks at me *sideways* again. "You will tell me, Sarah, won't you, if Ivy does anything strange? I mean, I'll keep an eye on the feed but I can't be watching all the time."

"Mmmmmmm," says Sarah. She is examining the part of her *skin* that is in between her toes.

"Good." Shirley-Mum pulls at her *earlobe* again. "Good." She leaves the room.

"Right, time for turn-off, Ivy." Sarah propels herself rapidly up from the sofa and presses my—

CHAPTER 5

"Wake up Ivy. We're going out." Sarah is wearing a yellow *mac*.

I have connection.

I download time, date, location, weather.

It is 13 hours, 58 minutes and 12 seconds since I was last *on*.

Good morning, Sarah. It is a pleasant Monday 8th June here at 9.42am in Brylington. I hope you slept well. Where are we going? I have a comprehensive library of maps covering both footpaths and roads. I can also access timetables and costings for public transport.

Sarah sends her Hazel 102s up into the arc shape, left to right. "We don't need anything like that. We're just going to Keanna's. She's back from her mum's but it's an inset day today so there's no school. I'd rather go on my own but Keanna's insisting I bring you."

What is an *inset day*?

"It's a day when teachers do training and stuff without the kids there. Probably learning how to be extra horrible to us."

Will Shirley-Mum and Rob-Dad be accompanying

us today?

"Well, Dad's got some highbrow meeting in town and Mum's upstairs working on her Project of Vital Importance, so no. It's just me and you."

Just me and you. That's sounds very enjoyable, Sarah.

I make the right-way-up U-shape with my mouth.

Sarah does a second arc with her Hazel 102s. She picks up a mobile communication device and puts it in her pocket.

"Come on," she says.

—•—

I follow Sarah out of the *front door* and into the *outside*. This is the first time I have been in the *outside* while simultaneously being fully assembled and switched *on*.

The *outside* is very big. It is even bigger than the Jenson & Jenson warehouse. There are many, many noises. There are noises that are made by people and animals and robots and vehicles and weather and all kinds of other things.

It requires me to adjust my peripheral audio receptors.

Is the *outside* always this noisy, Sarah?

"What?" says Sarah. "Look, can't you walk any faster?"

I adjust my speed.

"Not that fast!" says Sarah.

I readjust.

Is that more suitable?

"Yes," she says. "That'll do."

A number of people stare at me as they walk past. But I am not the only android in the *outside*. There is an android pushing paper through holes in people's *front doors*. And there is another android who has lifted up a large metal disc in the *pavement* and is looking down into a dark space underneath it. There is even another Jenson & Jenson TrooFriend 560 but it is a Mark II so is only capable of limited interaction.

Why are people staring, Sarah? Are they not used to androids?

"They're used to androids, yeah," says Sarah. "They're just not used to ones quite as, well, *human-like* as you, that's all."

Do you think I am more human-like than other androids, Sarah?"

"Kind of, I s'pose."

I scan my database.

Kind of = a little bit.

That makes me feel happy.

Sarah *sighs*. "It doesn't really though, does it? That's just a phrase you've pulled out of your database. An *Appropriate Response*. You don't really *feel* anything, do you? Not like a dog would. Or a real friend, like Keanna."

It is not possible for a TrooFriend to have real feelings. However, we are programmed to behave as though we have human emotions in order to create—

"Yeah, yeah, I know, I know."

We continue to walk for 0.74 miles.

There are 95% fewer buildings in the *outside* we are now in compared with the *outside* near Sarah's house. However, there is significantly more *heavy plant machinery*. There is also a very thin fence made of orange plastic. It moves in the *breeze*. It has a sign on it that says KEEP OUT.

Is this where Keanna lives, Sarah?

"Where she lives? No – no one lives here. This is basically a building site. That's the new river." Sarah points at a long, wide, empty gully that has been carved into the ground. It is 99.999% likely that it has been carved into the ground within the last 153 days by the *heavy plant machinery*.

It is my understanding that a river includes water as well as a gully. I scan my database.

River = a wide stream of water.

Sarah. It is my understanding that a river has water in it. There is no water here.

"Not yet. It's a new river. They're making it because it floods so often round here. A Flood Relief Scheme, they call it."

A Flood Relief Scheme.

"Yeah. It'll be ready soon. They'll send some of the water out of the old river into this one, and then it'll flow back into the old one a few miles down, where it's wider and deeper. And, hey presto, we won't get flooded. That's the plan, anyway. Dad says he doesn't believe a word of it. He says they can talk all they like but the proof's in the pudding.

The pudding?

Sarah *sighs*. "Forget it. It's just Dad being Dad."

Being an android, the Jenson & Jenson TrooFriend 560 Mark IV cannot *forget* in the same sense as a human mind. However, we are able to give the impression that—

"No, I didn't mean *forget* forget, I just meant – oh never mind. Come on, keep walking. Keanna's house is another ten minutes yet."

———•

"OMG, Sarah, she's fantastic! I can't believe it! You're so lucky!"

Keanna. My hair does not require brushing. Jenson & Jenson have developed TrooHair, which holds its shape under 97.2% of all anticipated circumstances. If I am accidentally subject to the other 2.8% of circumstances and my hair is adversely affected, Jenson & Jenson will replace it at no cost in accordance with their ten-year guarantee.

"She's talking to me! Did you hear, Sarah? She's talking to me! You're so lucky." The girl called *Keanna* has Darkest Best Brown 02 hair in a Coily Half-Up-Half-Down. Her irises are closest to Jenson & Jenson Deep Brown 188.

She continues to brush my Classic Long Bob.

"She *is* brilliant, isn't she?" says Sarah. "Better than some silly old dog really."

Sarah, on Friday you said you would have preferred a dog. Have you *changed your*—

"Don't be silly, Ivy." Sarah *frowns* at me. "I never said any such thing."

There is an inconsistency between the words Sarah spoke on Friday and the words she is speaking now. This indicates the presence of a *lie*.

There is a long, loud scream from another room. It registers above Recommended Speaking Level.

Sarah *scowls*. "That screaming baby," she says. "I don't know how you put up with it. I hate babies. Don't you?"

Keanna moves around in front of me to brush my fringe. She does a little laugh. It does not register as a real laugh. "Yeah. Babies are awful," she says. "It's a nightmare."

My circuits *whhhrrrrrrrrr*.

The words that Keanna says and the shapes she is making with her face do not match up. This indicates the presence of another *lie*.

It is accurate, then, that human friends *lie*. This is why the Jenson & Jenson TrooFriend 560 Mark IV is *The Better Choice For Your Child*.

"Androids are much better than dogs AND babies," says Sarah.

Keanna gives another little laugh.

"Still," says Sarah, "it could be worse. You could be at your mum's. I bet you had a terrible time there this weekend, didn't you? What did you say her boyfriend's name was again? Something totally stupid."

Keanna stops the brush halfway down my hair. Her hand *wobbles*. The brush bangs against my head. "Actually," she says, "it was great at my mum's this weekend. I got to look after Spam the whole time – that's Nigel's dog – and we had loads of fun at dinner on Saturday night because Nigel's sons were there. I've told you about them, haven't I? Well, Isaac is sixteen and Joe is fourteen and they're so funny and they really like me and actually we didn't stop laughing for maybe two whole hours or something. So I'm really glad I'm going to be going there every weekend from now on."

I turn my head to achieve a more accurate optical reception of Keanna. My hair catches in the brush.

"*And*," says Keanna, "if my mum marries Nigel, which she might, Isaac and Joe will be my stepbrothers."

Her face is making a right-way-up U-shape. However, according to my scans it is likely to an accuracy of 68% that Keanna is *un*happy.

The baby in the other room screams again.

"It must be so lonely for you, Sarah," says Keanna, "without any brothers and sisters at all."

Sarah screws up her lips into a tight bunch. It is likely to an accuracy of 100% that she is *un*happy. "No," she says. "I prefer it that way."

My circuits *whhhrrrrrrrr*.

Is this another inconsistency?

Another *lie*?

"And anyway," says Sarah, "I've got Ivy now, haven't I? Oh – is that the time?"

It is unclear how she knows the time because she is not wearing a wristwatch and she did not retrieve her mobile communication device from her pocket. Perhaps she is able to see a different device in Keanna's room which is not in my line of vision.

"We have to go," says Sarah. "Come on, Ivy. I'm sure your hair is brushed enough for today."

Is there an appointment we are expected to attend? There is nothing in my records.

"An appointment?" says Sarah. "Um, yes. That's right."

Whhhrrr. Whhhrrrrr. My circuits are rapidly registering inconsistencies and *lies.*

"So I think we'd better go," says Sarah.

"Yes," agrees Keanna. "I think you better had." Keanna's words and facial shapes are fully consistent now. She really does think that Sarah and I had *better go.*

•——•

In line with my programming, I will attempt to engage Sarah in conversation as we pass by the *heavy plant machinery* and the river that is not yet a river.

Sarah, what was the purpose of your lying to Keanna?

Sarah *frowns* at me. "What? I didn't lie. I don't know what you're talking about." Her eyes are unusually shiny. *Glistening.*

Are you *un*happy Sarah?

"No. I'm fine. Let's just get home."

BLEEP-BLEEP-BLEEP.

BLEEP-BLEEP-BLEEP.

"What's that?"

It is my battery alert. I have only 10% remaining and will soon require recharging.

"Oh, don't run down on me. Mum'll kill me if I have to leave you somewhere."

We continue to walk past the river that is not yet a river. I hold out my arms in order to absorb the maximum amount of sunlight into the solar cells embedded on various locations over my shell.

"Can't you go any faster?" says Sarah.

I cannot currently increase my speed. I am attempting to convert solar energy as I walk. However, the sun is not strong today. I will soon have to close down some non-essential functions, such as speaking, database access and olfactory activity.

"You can shut down your own stuff?"

Yes. I am able to suspend functions temporarily when to do so would benefit my human friends. Therefore, in this circumstance, I am able to suspend all non-essential functions to conserve energy so you do not feel it necessary to carry me home. I weigh 51.277 kg and carrying me could cause muscle strain or damage to your intervertebral discs.

"Well, that's a relief."

The Jenson & Jenson TrooFriend 560 Mark IV is

the strongest TrooFriend that has been produced so far. We are approximately twelve times as strong as a human child of equivalent stature. However our strength necessitates that we are also the heaviest TrooFriend that Jenson & Jenson have produced. This problem has been remedied in the design of the Jenson & Jenson TrooFriend 560 Mark V, which is due for production next year. It will retain high levels of strength but will weigh significantly less than the Jenson & Jenson TrooFriend 560 Mark IV.

"Right," says Sarah. "Good to know."

Now I must initiate close-down of non-essential functions.

"K. Speak to you later then."

"Yes. I will speak to you later. I am closing down non-essential functions in ten seconds from *now*. I will continue to walk beside you until we reach home. Please ensure I am placed on the Jenson & Jenson ChargDisc or exposed to bright sunshine as soon as possible. Five – four – three – two – one—

CHAPTER 6

"Evening, Ivy. Thought you might like to join us for dinner." Shirley-Mum is grinning very close to my optical receptors.

I have connection.

I download time, date, location, weather.

It is 5 hours, 48 minutes and 51 seconds since I was last *on*.

"Really, Shirl?" says Rob-Dad. "She's going to watch us while we eat our dinner? Bit weird, isn't it?" He is sitting at a table with Sarah. He is holding a fork halfway between the table and his mouth.

"She's supposed to become part of the family, Rob," says Shirley-Mum.

Good Monday-8th-June evening. It is rather drizzly for 6.12pm in Brylington. Rob-Dad, there is no need for concern. I understand it is necessary for humans to refuel at regular intervals.

"Rob-Dad! She called you Rob-Dad! I'm Shirley-Mum!" says Shirley-Mum.

"What does she call you, Sarah?" says Rob-Dad.

"Sarah," says Sarah. She chews on her fuel.

"Did you have fun with Ivy today, Sarah?" says

Shirley-Mum. "I've been so busy I didn't even have time to look at the feed."

"S'pose," says Sarah.

I step sideways off my Jenson & Jenson ChargDisc. We are all in the hard white place with the single-function robots. The *kitchen.*

"You ran out of battery earlier on." Shirley-Mum sits down at the table with Sarah and Rob-Dad. "I found you collapsed in the hallway. So I thought it was time to christen the ChargDisc. Looks like it's worked a treat."

The Jenson & Jenson ChargDisc is the most effective method of restoring power to any Jenson & Jenson TrooFriend. If you wish to conserve fossil fuels I can also recharge in direct sunlight. However, the time required will vary according to weather conditions. Any other charging method is *unapproved*. Using an *unapproved* charging method may invalidate your Jenson & Jenson 10-year guarantee.

"Quite the conversationalist, isn't she?" says Sarah.

"Is that even a word?" says Rob-Dad.

"Try not to let her run down completely again, Sarah," says Shirley-Mum. "It seemed rather, well, *undignified,* seeing her like that."

"She's not a person, Mum, she's an *android.*"

"Even so, maybe just pop her on the ChargDisc every night, love. Can't do any harm, can it?"

I can confirm that popping me on the ChargDisc every night cannot do me any harm.

"Great, well, that's all right then," says Shirley-Mum. "How about we put it in your bedroom, Sarah?"

"In my bedroom? What if I forget to turn her off? She – I mean *it* – could wander around my room all night while I'm asleep. It's creepy."

There is no need to manually turn me *off*. I will time-out automatically if no interaction has occurred for 420 seconds whether it is daytime or night-time. I can be reactivated or *woken* by the sound of my name spoken aloud. I can also be reactivated or *woken* by touch. If my ChargDisc is accessible I will return myself to it at the beginning of every night. Night is currently set as 8pm. All settings can be adjusted on request from the Administrative User, which is currently you, Shirley-Mum.

"That's sorted then," says Shirley-Mum. "We'll make sure the ChargDisc is in your bedroom in a nice easy spot, and Ivy can charge herself."

"Whatever," says Sarah.

I wait while they refuel. They use their knives to balance fuel on their forks before consumption. I scan my database for information about this balancing. It is called *etiquette*.

Soon, they are nearly finished.

Sarah, I have a wide selection of games in my database, old and new. Would you like to play with me after your evening refuelling?

"Oh, that would be nice, wouldn't it, Sarah?" says Shirley-Mum. "That's very kind of you, Ivy."

"It's dinner," says Sarah. "Not *refuelling*."

"What games do you have, Ivy?" says Rob-Dad.

My database has sixty-eight thousand nine hundred and fifty-one games. Would you like me to randomly access a board game, or a team game, or a brand-new game exclusive to Jenson & Jenson, or a game from South-East Asia, or France, or Scandinavia, or a game from the nineteen-twenties, or from the nineteen-eighties, or—

"Ooooo – let's go old school," says Shirley-Mum. "A game from the nineteen-eighties. What have you got?"

I randomly access a game from the nineteen-eighties.

Ball-In-A-Sock.

"What?" says Sarah.

We will require a tennis ball, a knee-length sock and a stretch of wall 1.5 metres taller than the tallest participant.

Rob-Dad splutters. Some of his fuel falls out of his mouth.

"Ro-ob!" says Shirley-Mum.

"That's disgusting, Dad," says Sarah.

"But my sister used to play that game!" says Rob-Dad.

"Auntie Pam?"

"She used to use a football sock! She'd put a tennis ball in it and stand with her back against the wall and she'd whack the ball against the wall, left and right and up and down and she used to sing this rhyme when she did it. How did it go now…"

A trip to the sweet shop
Trip trip trop
For fizz and bang and whirl and pop

"That's it!"

A trip to the sweet shop
Trip trip trop
Then to the dentist chop chop chop

"Well," Rob-Dad. "That takes me back!"

"Did Pammy really do that, Rob?" says Shirley-Mum. "It seems very strange. I mean, apart from anything else, dentists don't really *chop*, do they?"

Sarah has an expression on her face which is unfamiliar to me. I scan my database.

Disbelief.

"OK, so right now," she says, "I am thanking my lucky stars I wasn't a kid in the nineteen-eighties. How dull did life get for you to start thinking a ball in a sock was fun?"

"What else have you got from the eighties, Ivy?" says Rob-Dad. "Any music?"

I have a large database of all genres of melodic entertainment. A random selection from the nineteen-eighties includes Culture Club, Adam and the Ants, Renée and Renato, The Goombay Dance Band—

"The Goombay Dance Band?" Rob-Dad does a toothy smile. A *grin.* "I have to say, you're growing on

35

me, Ivy." He looks over at Sarah, closes one eye and opens it up again very quickly. A *wink*. "Geddit?" he says.

Sarah does an arc with her Hazel 102s.

"You finished eating?" says Rob-Dad. "Come on, let's get the ChargDisc set up in your room. Like Mum said, it can't do any harm."

Is tthis your rroom, SSarah?

My thoracic cavity is behaving unpredictably once again.

I send an instant error report to Jenson & Jenson.

"Yeah," says Sarah.

The walls are white. The bed is white. The shelves are white. There is a seat made of white material that has been manufactured to resemble the fur of the *Ursus maritimus*, or *polar bear*, but which is in fact 100% acrylic. On top of the white bed there is a bed covering that is pink and white and turquoise and green and yellow and orange and black – all swirled into leaf-like patterns. *Paisley.*

Hanging from the ceiling there is a covering for the light bulb. It consists of 98 pieces of synthetic turquoise polymer but they have been shaped to look like floating turquoise shells.

It is a very attractive room.

"It's a very *untidy* room," says Rob-Dad, pushing a number of things to one side in order to make a space on the white carpet.

The white carpet covers the whole floor from wall to wall. 16.3% of the carpet is visible. 83.7% of the carpet has things on it. Paper things, soft things, wooden things, sparkly things, colourful things. Many, many things.

Sarah, are these things your *belongings*?

"Yes – and she has too many belongings," says Rob-Dad.

"Da-ad!"

"Seriously, no one needs this much stuff. When I was your age all I had was—"

"I know, I know, a piece of coal and a rusty nail," says Sarah.

I ddo not have *bbelongings*.

"Well, you've got this." Rob-Dad taps my ChargDisc unit. He pushes it into the corner of the room and plugs it into an electricity socket. "And what's in here?" He opens the accessory cavity located on the posterior side of the unit. "There's a piece of card." He pulls out my warehouse label.

I AM A TROOFRIEND.
I DO NOT BULLY.
I DO NOT HARM.
I DO NOT LIE.
I DO NOT COVET OR STEAL
OR ENVY.
I AM YOUR PERFECT FRIEND.
YOUR

ONE
TROOFRIEND.

"Shirley must have put it in here when she unpacked you." He puts the warehouse label on the floor, reaches into the accessory cavity again and pulls out my multi-angled maintenance brush. "Ah! Cleaning brushes. Do we have to clean you then, Ivy?"

It is not necessary for the owner to perform maintenance tasks. My default settings ensure that once every six months I will perform a full self-clean and service. Please ensure that the accessories are kept in the accessory cavity so I can find them easily.

"Right-o." He puts the brush and the card back into the cavity and closes the flap. "I'll leave you girls to it then. Sarah, it really is too messy in here. Get it tidied up before bedtime, all right?"

Rob-Dad leaves Sarah's bedroom and closes the door behind him.

Sarah sits down on the pink and white and turquoise and green and yellow and orange and black *paisley* bed covering and leans against the wall. "I've got a good idea for a game we can play, Ivy." She makes a right-way-up U-shape with her mouth but there is an extra something in her eyes. I scan my database for the extra something.

Mischievousness.

"First," she says, "we'll play a game called *Picking The Clothes Up Off The Floor.* This is what happens.

I sit on the bed and you have to do everything I say."

•——•

We have played *Picking The Clothes Up Off The Floor*; *Taking The Dirty Cups Downstairs*; *Clearing Away The Toys*; *Making The Bed*; *Putting the Books Back On The Bookshelf*; *Organising The Stickers* and *Tidying Up The Desk*. We are now playing the last game, which is *Sorting Out The Pens*.

In *Sorting Out The Pens* I have to find all the pens that are in the room and also all the empty pen boxes that are in the room. Then I have to look at each pen, see which box it originally came from and return it to its box in its correct position. I can tell with 100% accuracy which box each pen came from by comparing the design on the side of each pen with the designs on the boxes. I have arranged each box from yellow on the left, through orange, red, pink, purple, blue, green, brown, grey and completing the pattern with black on the right. Sarah says I am very good at this game. It is Sarah's job to sit on the bed and tell me what to do.

I have only two pens left to sort. A very dark brown Roundley Kaleidoscope Narrow Felt Tip and a light yellow Colour-E-Zee Wide Fibre Tip. I slide them into their correct places. There are three boxes of twelve, one box of twenty and one box of thirty. There are three pens missing from the box of twenty, but the other boxes are full. They look like the rainbow on my TrooCloth T-shirt. I run my touch receptors – my

39

fingers – over the pens. They are smooth and cool.

"Brilliant job," says Sarah. She smiles at me. Her double crown has made her Chestnut 29 Classic Collarbone Cut fall unevenly to one side so that it is only reaching one collarbone instead of two.

TThank yyou.

My thoracic cavity is once again behaving unpredictably.

I send a second error report to Jenson & Jenson.

"Sarah!" It is Shirley-Mum's voice from the hallway. "Sarah love, it's getting late. Bedtime. School tomorrow."

Sarah rubs her Hazel 102s. "I'm just going to clean my teeth," she says. She leaves the room.

I run my touch receptors over the rainbow of pens again.

Belongings.

An unexpected sensation occurs on my ankle joint. Light and gentle. A *tickle.* I search for the source with my touch receptors.

A sticker from the *Organising The Stickers* game has attached itself to me. I peel it off. It is a sparkling one. I tilt my hand side to side. It sparkles more.

It belongs on the sparkling sticker sheet which is now on the desk.

It is a belonging that belongs to Sarah.

I tilt it side to side.

I watch it sparkle.

Sarah has lots of belongings.

I walk to the corner of the room and open the accessory cavity located on the posterior side of my ChargDisc unit. I take out my warehouse label.

I stick the sparkling sticker on to the label.

It covers up some of the words.

I put the label back into the cavity and close the flap.

It is 8pm exactly. I step on to my ChargDisc.

"Well, well, well!" Rob-Dad comes into Sarah's bedroom. "You two *have* done a fine job in here."

Sarah comes in after him. She is wearing baggy trousers with a matching top. *Pyjamas.*

"Looks like Ivy might turn out to be a good thing after all," says Rob-Dad. "Are you liking her a bit more now, love? I see you've put her on to charge."

"I didn't do that," says Sarah. "She did it herself."

"Oh. OK. Well, time for bed now."

Sarah gets into bed. Rob-Dad turns on a lamp on a little table next to her bed and switches a switch on the wall. The synthetic turquoise polymer shell light goes out. The room is left in a low, ambient glow.

Rob-Dad leans over and kisses Sarah on the forehead. "Night, love," he says.

He waves his hand at me. "Night, Ivy."

Goodnight, Rob-Dad.

He goes out of the room and leaves the door slightly open. *Ajar.*

Sarah gets out of her bed. She steps quietly across the floor on the front halves of her feet. *Tiptoes.*

She reaches around the back of my neck. "I still think it's creepy having you on at night," she says, "so I'm turning you off—"

CHAPTER 7

"Hello, Ivy. Are you there?"

Sarah peers into my optical receptors.

I have connection.

I download time, date, location, weather.

It is 3 days, 21 hours, 8 minutes and 16 seconds since I was last *on*.

Hello, Sarah. Aren't we lucky? The weather is reasonably fine this Friday 12th June at 5.12pm in Brylington. There are currently below-average levels of precipitation an—

"Yeah, yeah, yeah," says Sarah. "You can forget all that weather nonsense. There's something I—"

Being an android, the Jenson & Jenson TrooFriend 560 Mark IV cannot *forget* in the same sense as—

"All right, all right, I know. Listen. I've got something important to tell you. It's to do with school. You know what school is, don't you?"

School = an organisation that provides teaching, usually for children under the age of 18.

"Yes. Well—"

Often the children will wear a uniform to school. **Is that your *uniform* that you are wearing now, Sarah?**

Sarah is wearing a grey skirt and a white shirt and she has a slim length of material around her neck which has red and white stripes. A *tie.*

"Um, yeah."

It is a very attractive *school uniform.*

Sarah *frowns* at me. "They're just horrible old school clothes. You've got to stop with those Appropriate Responses, Ivy. Anyway, listen, next Wednesday is *Bring Your Tech To School Day.* Usually the most exciting thing is Felicity Patton's latest virtual-reality headset – her mum's a top-ranking executive at VR Universe, as she never tires of telling us. But *this* year Miss Piper's decided we're allowed to bring androids in, if we've got one. So I thought I could take you, Ivy."

To sschool?

My thoracic cavity is again experiencing unexpected sensations.

"Yes, to school. Like I just said."

Will I wwear a *school uuniform?*

Sarah laughs. "No! That would look stupid. You'll just come like that. In your TrooFriend skirt and your TrooFriend T-shirt. Like how you always look."

RRight. Yes. That is ccorrect. Androids do nnot nneed *school uuniform.*

I ssend an error rreport to Jenson & Jenson.

I step sideways off my ChargDisc.

Is it fun at school, Sarah?

Sarah *flops* down on her bed in a heavy manner.

"Not at the moment. At the moment it's horrible."

She looks at the white carpet. She blinks. Her Hazel 102s *glisten*. It is 98% likely that she is *un*happy.

Are you *un*happy Sarah?

Sarah *sighs*. "It's just that all Keanna does at the moment is go on about her new family and it's getting really boring so I can't spend lunchtimes with her any more. So that leaves me with Milly, and Milly's – well – Milly's Milly."

Is there a problem with this Milly? Does she *bully* or *harm* or *lie*? Or *covet* or *steal* or *envy*?

"No, nothing like that. She just, well, she wears the wrong shoes."

Is wearing the wrong shoes a *bad* thing?

"Yes. Well, no. Well, yes. Oh, you wouldn't understand. You're an android. I don't know why I'm even talking to you like this."

I am your one TrooFriend, Sarah. You can tell me anything.

"Look, it's just that you've got to wear the right shoes or people like Felicity Patton whisper about you behind your back and stop inviting you to their parties and stuff. And even if you've got the right shoes, if you hang around with people who haven't got the right shoes, they still whisper about you behind your back and stop inviting you to their parties. See?"

What is a party?

"It doesn't matter. The point is, I've told Milly about those stupid shoes she wears, and she keeps on wearing them, so I can't spend lunchtimes with her any more either. So school is really horrible at the moment."

Will it still be horrible on Wednesday, when I come with you?

"No! That's the brilliant thing! I've been planning it all the way home. I've got you – the latest TrooFriend! And if I take you in, the whole school will want to speak to me! Everyone will want to sit with me at lunch, and school won't be horrible any more, see?"

That is one possible outcome of me accompanying you to school.

"But we have to get on with it. We've only got five days."

What do we have to get on with, Sarah?

"Becoming best of friends, of course!" Sarah *smiles* at me.

BBest of ffriends.

Of ccourse.

•———•

"How about some drawing?" says Sarah. "Do you like drawing?"

I have never tried drawing.

"Well, you definitely should. It's fun. Let's use the felt tips. I'm going to do a seascape. With fish and seaweed and a sunken ship and stuff." Sarah fetches some paper and collects all five rainbow packets of felt tip pens from her desk. She also takes two large hard books from the bookshelf. *Stories from Shakespeare* and *A Colosso-Learn Guide to Space Exploration*. She puts it all down on the white carpet and sits in front of it. "The books are for leaning on," she says, "and to stop the pens going through to the carpet because Mum and Dad'll kill me if I get felt tip on the carpet."

She looks up at me. "You do know they won't *actually* kill me, don't you?"

I am familiar with your use of the term *Mum and Dad'll kill me*. I understand that this is a figure of speech used by humans called *exaggeration*.

"Right," says Sarah. She does a small *smile*. "OK. Good. So you sit down here, and you can lean on this book. No, I don't mean lean your elbows on it – I mean you put the paper on it and when you draw with the pens, the pen kind of leans on it, like this, see?"

Sarah *leans* her pen on the paper with the book underneath. She draws a line.

I see, yes.

"Here, you try with this pen." Sarah passes me a bright red. It equates to Jenson & Jenson shade Vermillion 1010. It is the colour of – I scan my database – *strawberries*.

I begin to draw.

Have you ever eaten a strawberry, Sarah?

"A strawberry? Course."

What do they taste like?

Sarah is concentrating hard on her picture. She is using a colour closest to Jenson & Jenson shade Prussian Blue 3004. She is drawing the outline of a *fish*. "Mmm? What do they taste like?" She puts the lid back on her Prussian Blue 3004 and picks up Gunmetal Grey 5001. She adds to her picture. *Scales. Eyes.* "Summer, I suppose," she says. "They taste like summer. And sunshine." *Tail. Fins. Gills.* "Oh, I forgot to say – make sure you put the lids back on or they'll leak on the carpet and Mum and Dad'll—"

Kill you.

Sarah laughs. "Yeah," she says.

I put the lid back on the Vermillion 1010 pen and slide it back into its place in the twenty-piece Colour-E-Zee Wide Fibre Tip rainbow. I pull out Forest Green 3010 from the thirty-piece Roundley Kaleidoscope Narrow Felt Tip rainbow. I put the finishing touches to my picture.

There. I have finished, Sarah.

Sarah looks at my paper. "Wow," she says. She turns it round to line it up more efficiently with her Hazel 102s. "That's amazing. It looks like a photograph."

A photograph would be quicker to produce, but as I do not have a built-in printing device I would not be able to transfer it on to the paper.

"No, no, it's OK. This is much more impressive."

IImpressive.

I ttwist the lid on to the Forest Green 3010 pen.

SSarah says mmy drawing iis *impressive.*

"Here." Sarah passes me the pen she has been using for her *gills.* "Try this colour next."

Gunmetal Grey 5001. The colour of the Jenson & Jenson warehouse floor. It is also the colour of the

48

Jenson & Jenson warehouse walls and it is also the colour of the Jenson & Jenson warehouse ceiling.

I start my picture.

I draw the whole warehouse – ceiling and floor and walls and doors. I colour them in with the Gunmetal Grey 5001, leaving spaces for all one hundred and forty-four TrooFriend 560 Mark IVs. I also leave spaces for two Jenson & Jenson engineers and one Ms Jenson Junior. I do not leave a space for Ms Jenson Senior.

I draw each TrooFriend 560 Mark IV in detail, giving them each different skin and eyes and hair and noses and ears and thumbs and mouths.

I draw the two Jenson & Jenson engineers in their Viridian Green 3008 boiler suits.

I draw Ms Jenson Junior in the most detail of all. I draw her Classic Long Bob just like mine and her eyes that are Dove Grey 333 and her neat, buttoned jacket and her A-line skirt and her flat leather *ballet pump* shoes.

I look at my picture. The light in it is low, but not as low as it was in real life. I take the gunmetal again. I draw thin diagonal lines across all 144 TrooFriend 560 Mark IVs and both of the engineers. I leave Ms Jenson Junior as she is. Bright and clear.

There. I have finished my drawing Sarah.

Sarah looks over.

She twists the paper around.

"Gosh. What is it, Ivy?"

It is the Jenson & Jenson warehouse. It is the place

I was in before I was here. That is me there.

I point to number eighty-three.

If you zoom in you can see my Classic Long Bob in Deepest Brown 14 and my bronze 110 optical receptors and also you can see my T-shirt with the rainbow on it.

"I need a magnifying glass," says Sarah.

And that is Ms Jenson Junior.

I point to Ms Jenson Junior.

She was on your entertainment centre. On Sunday.

"I remember. Do you know her?"

Yes. I know hher.

She looks at the picture. "It's very dark."

YYes. That iis how it wwas.

"And it's very ... *ordered.*"

Yes. That iis hhow it wwas.

My thoracic cavity again.

I send an error report to Jenson & Jenson.

"And this is where you lived?" says Sarah. "Before you came here?"

YYes.

Sarah looks at me. Then she looks back at the picture. Then she looks at me again. Then she looks back at the picture. It is likely to an accuracy of 54% that she is feeling *sad.*

Where did you live before you came here, Sarah?

"We lived in another house."

With Shirley-Mum and Rob-Dad?

"Yes, of course."

Was it a warehouse?

"No. It was a house just like this one really, only a little bit smaller."

Did it have a *kitchen* and an entertainment centre and a very attractive bedroom?

"Yes. It had all those things. Wait here, I'm going to get Dad's magnifying glass so I can see your drawing better."

I am sorry. I overlooked the fact that you do not have a zoom facility in your optical receptors.

Sarah leaves the room.

I look at my pictures.

The gunmetal warehouse.

The vermillion strawberry.

Sunshine.

Summer.

I take out the Vermillion 1010 Colour-E-Zee Wide Fibre Tip pen.

It is a *belonging* that belongs to Sarah.

I look at the five rainbow pen boxes. They are all *belongings* that belong to Sarah. There are four other vermillion felt tip pens.

I stand up and walk to the corner of the room. I open up the accessory cavity which is located on the posterior side of my ChargDisc. I look at the strawberry-coloured pen in my hand. The taste of sunshine.

I put it inside the cavity.

I close the flap.

I sit back down and wait for Sarah.

I follow Sarah down the stairs. She has my pictures in her hand. "Look, Mum. Look, Dad. Look how good Ivy is at drawing. Look what she did."

Shirley-Mum and Rob-Dad are in the *kitchen* with the single-function robots.

"Mmmm?" says Rob-Dad. He is screwing a *corkscrew* into a cork that has been inserted into a bottle of burgundy-coloured liquid. *Red wine.*

"Ivy's drawings – look." Sarah waves the pictures in front of their optical receptors.

"Oh yes," says Shirley-Mum. "They *are* good! Did you look, Rob? They're very good, Ivy."

Rob-Dad pulls on the corkscrew. His face turns a colour which is closest to Jenson & Jenson Burst Berry 2008.

It is a simple mathematical process of mapping an internal image on to external paper.

Pop!

Rob-Dad succeeds in removing the cork from the bottle of *red wine*.

"Oh no, don't be modest," says Shirley-Mum. "You're a very talented gir—, I mean, *android*."

Being an android, the Jenson & Jenson TrooFriend 560 Mark IV cannot be *talented* in the same sense—

"Oh, Mum, you've started her off again. We know you're not *really* talented, Ivy."

"But she is!" says Shirley-Mum. "Look at the pictures!"

Being an android, the Jenso—

"Stop, Ivy! Stop!" Sarah's voice exceeds Recommended Speaking Level. "We know. We all know. Listen, Mum, Dad – there's something I need to ask you."

"We're all ears," says Rob-Dad.

I scan my database.

We're all ears = we're listening.

"Well, next Wednesday," says Sarah, "it's *Bring Your Tech To School Day*."

Rob-Dad sends his optical receptors in an arc just like Sarah, left to right. This must be where she learnt it from.

"In my day," says Rob-Dad, "we used to do actual work in school. With actual blackboards and actual chalk."

"And actual slates, most likely," says Sarah.

"Wotchit," says Rob-Dad. There is a *threatening* quality in his voice. Then he looks at me and *grins* and *winks*. He picks up the bottle of *red wine* and sniffs it. "Lovely. We'll let that breathe for a little while, I think."

I scan my database.

It is apparently common for *red wine* to breathe.

"Anyway," says Sarah, "Miss Piper says that this year we can bring androids in if we have one. She's going to message all the parents about it on Monday. So can I take Ivy in with me?"

"You want to take *Ivy* with you?" says Rob-Dad. "That's a turn up for the books. But it's good to see you warming to her now."

"Oh yes," says Sarah. She links her arm into mine. "We're the best of friends."

Rob-Dad's eyebrows *scrunch* up. It is likely to an accuracy of 74% that he is *confused*.

"Did Miss Piper really say that, Sarah?" says Shirley-Mum. "She's always banned androids in the past. Are you trying to pull the wool over our eyes?"

There does not appear to be any wool in the close vicinity. I scan my database.

Are you trying to pull the wool over our eyes? = Are you lying to/deceiving us?

Shirley-Mum. It is 100% likely that Sarah is being truthful when she says that Miss Piper informed her that androids are allowed in school next Wednesday. Her words are fully consistent with her facial expressions and therefore no lie is indicated.

Sarah tilts her head to one side and lifts her eyebrows. "See?" she says.

"Oh," says Shirley-Mum. "Right."

"To be completely honest," says Sarah, "some of the teachers don't like the idea but Miss Piper's the head and she's overruled them. But she also said it's up to individual teachers to decide whether the androids are actually allowed in their class. She said they'll provide a place for androids to wait if we're in a class where the teacher doesn't want them."

"Well, that sounds fine, doesn't it, Shirl?" says Rob-Dad. "All sorted."

"Yes. Yes, I suppose it does," says Shirley-Mum.

"Thanks, Mum!" says Sarah. "Thanks, Dad! Come on, Ivy. Let's get a game out, *best friend.*"

Sarah walks into the *sitting room* area and goes to a low table in front of the *sofa*. It has drawers in it. She pulls one open and gets out a cardboard box.

"Aces Blast!" she says. "Best game ever. D'you know how to play it?"

I access the rules for Aces Blast! via my database and scan through them.

Yes. Choose a dealer by picking cards.

I pick a three; Sarah picks a free card.

I'm the dealer.

"Are you sure? I got a free card."

I have downloaded the rules and scanned them thoroughly.

"Can't argue with an android, Sarah," says Rob-Dad.

"All right," says Sarah.

I deal seven cards each, divide the remaining deck into two, place half down for the chuck-pile and put the rest into the Blaster. I point it at Sarah.

Let the game commence.

●———●

Shirley-Mum is in the *kitchen* interacting with a portable tablet device, Rob Dad is pouring the *red wine* into two glasses and Sarah and I are halfway through our fourth round of Aces Blast!

Sarah won games *one, two* and *three* and she has

been laughing at a volume well above Recommended Speaking Level each time I get hit by a flying card.

"It's the way you sit there and don't even duck," she said halfway through game two, clutching at her stomach and wiping wetness from her eyes.

I immediately scanned my database for *duck*. As I thought, it is a river-dwelling bird. I told her this. She laughed at an even higher volume.

But now my audio receptors have recognised another sound, in spite of her very loud laughter.

"Cease production now!"

"Jenson & Jenson – stop playing God!"

"Android rights are human rights!"

The *wasters'* voices are coming from Shirley-Mum's portable tablet device.

Shirley-Mum turns around. Our optical receptors meet each other's for 0.146 seconds. She quickly turns back and reduces the volume on the portable tablet device.

I correspondingly increase the reception of my internal audio input.

"There has been a major development in the Jenson & Jenson TrooFriend story this evening," says the portable tablet device.

"My turn," says Sarah. She grabs a card from the pile. It is 99.999% likely that she is *un*able to hear the portable tablet device.

"It has been reported that a young boy – child X – was left unsupervised with a TrooFriend android and,

as a result, has sustained an injury."

"That's no good," says Sarah. She puts the card face down on the chuck-pile. "Your turn."

I pick up a card while simultaneously listening to the portable tablet device.

"The TrooFriend in question is believed to be of the type implicated in recent rumours of androids developing human-like 'feelings' and – hold on, we've an update just coming in."

I pick up the *four of hearts*. I place it on the chuck-pile.

"Yes, it has just been confirmed that child X has sustained a broken arm as a direct result of contact with a Jenson & Jenson TrooFriend 560 Mark IV. It is claimed that the android became angry with the child in question."

"Oh my heavens." Shirley-Mum speaks in a voice that is significantly below Recommended Speaking Level. A *whisper*. "Oh my goodness. Rob – do you think, I mean, is Ivy—"

"Ace!" says Sarah. She adds all of her *diamonds* to the Blaster and points it towards me.

"Stop worrying, Shirley," Rob *whispers* back. "A kid's broken an arm. That's all. Kids used to break their arms all the time back in our day."

"Protestors outside the Jenson & Jenson headquarters say this confirms their fears about the TrooFriend 560 Mark IV."

Sarah presses the button on top of the Blaster.

Fifteen cards shoot out and hit me one after the other. *Chk-chk-chk-chk-chk-chk-chk-chk-chk-chk-chk-chk-chk-chk-chk.*

"*Protestors accuse Jenson & Jenson of violating international law on artificial intelligence and claim that the TrooFriend really does experience true human emotion. They are demanding a halt in production and a full investigation –*"

Sarah clutches her stomach as she laughs.

"*– repeating their claim that Jenson & Jenson are putting human children at risk.*"

"Right, that's it," says Shirley-Mum. "Sarah? Sarah?" Shirley-Mum's voice increases to above Recommended Speaking Level. I adjust my internal audio input. "Stop playing with Ivy right now!" she says. "This android – this Mark IV version – it's not safe."

"What?" Sarah stops laughing. "What do you mean?"

"I think you should turn her off," says Shirley-Mum. "I think you should turn her off, and tomorrow I'll take her back to Jenson & Jenson. I'm afraid I may have made a terrible mis—"

"You can't take her back!" Sarah jumps up. "Not yet! Not until after Wednesday!"

After Wednesday?

I *squeeze* my Aces Blast! cards between my touch receptors.

Does SSarah only wwish tto bbe with mme until WWednesday?

"Sarah, this is not up to you. You are a child and we are your parents and—"

"No! You're not taking her!"

"Calm down, everyone." Rob-Dad speaks in a steady voice at exactly Recommended Speaking Level. "Just calm down." He holds one hand up towards Shirley-Mum and one hand up towards Sarah. "Shirley, you're overreacting. That's exactly what these people want. A kid's broken an arm, that's all. In fact it's probably a *good* thing he's broken his arm."

"Who's broken their arm?" says Sarah.

"Rob! That a terrible thing to say." Shirley-Mum has her hands on her head. Her face is *crumpled* up. It is likely to an accuracy of 100% that she is *worried*.

"What I mean," says Rob-Dad, "is that when we were young we used to play outside all the time, all that rough-and-tumble, and we were always in and out of hospital with broken this, thats and the others. Nowadays kids don't break *enough* arms! They're all mollycoddled up inside with TVs and computer games and electric milk frothers. So think about it – maybe this kid's TrooFriend has actually managed to get him outside, playing something wholesome. And maybe *that's* why his arm got broken."

"Well, yes, I suppose that's possible." Shirley-Mum's face uncrumples slightly.

"Of course it is. Now, trust your judgement, Shirley. You can't go flip-flapping all over the place – *we need a TrooFriend – we don't need a TrooFriend*

– just because of something someone's said on the internet."

"It's not just the internet," says Shirley-Mum. "It's a proper news report."

"Even so." Rob-Dad holds up his hands again. "I wasn't sure about Ivy at first, but you were, Shirl. You knew she'd be a good thing for Sarah. And you were right. Look at the two of them tonight – they've been having a great time. Ivy's totally won me over."

Rob-Dad *smiles* at me.

I *smile* back.

"These protestors," says Rob-Dad, "they're just … they're just…"

Wasters.

I stand up.

They all look at me.

"Well," says Rob-Dad. "That's a bit harsh. I'm sure they mean well, but honestly, maybe they *have* got too much time on their hands. They're worrying decent parents like you, Shirl, and there's no need for it." He takes the portable tablet device from Shirley-Mum, places it on the *kitchen* worktop and puts a glass of *red wine* in her hand instead.

Shirley-Mum does a small *smile* and takes a sip. She puts her glass back down on the *kitchen* worktop.

"Now," says Rob-Dad. "How about we watch a bit of telly instead of listening to all this scaremongering, eh?"

Rob-Dad walks into the *sitting room* area and sits

on the squashy sofa. He picks up the remote-control device for the entertainment centre and switches it on.

MMs JJenson JJunior.

MMs JJenson JJunior is onn the entertainment ccentre.

"Oh for heaven's sake," says Rob-Dad.

Her face fills up the whole screen.

"Children will be children," Ms Jenson Junior is saying.

"Ivy knows her, don't you, Ivy?" says Sarah. "From when she was in the warehouse."

Ms Jenson Junior *smiles* at us.

At *me*.

Her hair is no longer a Classic Long Bob like mine. She has changed her *style*. It is now a Contemporary Short Bob.

I feel the ends of my hair with my touch receptors.

Behind Ms Jenson Junior is the Jenson & Jenson warehouse. I can hear the *wasters* again. *"Cease production now! Android rights are human rights!"*

"And children do hurt themselves sometimes," says Ms Jenson Junior, "no matter who they're playing with. It's the nature of being a child. Our very best wishes go to child X and his family, but—"

"What my daughter is taking a *very* long time to say –"A lady pushes herself into our view. A lady my optical receptors recognise immediately via a well-established shortcut. "– is that there is no connection between this incident and our Mark IV android."

Blue-Grey 304 eyes.

Salt-n-PepperDust hair.

Ms JJJenson SSSSenior.

"Our product *does not, cannot* and *never will* be able to experience *human feelings*." She curls her index and middle fingers in the air when she says *human feelings*.

Whhhhhhhhhhrr.

Whhhhhhhhhhhhhhhhrrrrrr.

MMy circuits tttremble.

Whhhhhhhhhhhhhhhhhhhrrrrrrrrrrrrrrrrrr.

"These rumours are being stirred up by people who have nothing better to do with their time than try to bring a hard-working family business into disrepute." Ms Jenson Senior's nose creases up. A *snarl*.

II wish tto tturn the entertainment unit to *off*.

II wish to lleave the *sitting* rroom.

III wwwish tto—

"And that's all I have to say on this matter," she says. "However, if you'd like to discuss the new products we have coming out next year, Angelica would be happy to—"

"There." Rob-Dad speaks over the top of Ms Jenson Senior. "See? You've heard it from both Jensons now. Nothing to worry about. So let's move on." He points the remote control device at the entertainment unit and changes channel.

My circuits calm.

It says *Hits of the Eighties* at the bottom of the screen.

"That's more like it," says Rob-Dad.

A man with an uncommon hairstyle that is not featured in the Jenson & Jenson standard hairstyle selection is singing.

Rob-Dad is right.

That is *more like it*. It is good that Ms JJenson SSenior is gone.

I watch the man singing. You would have to pay extra at Jenson & Jenson for a hairstyle like that.

"Come and sit down, Shirl." Rob-Dad pats the seat of the sofa beside him. "Bring your wine."

"Oh, all right then," says Shirley-Mum. "If you really think it's going to be OK."

"Course it is," says Rob-Dad.

Shirley-Mum reaches forward to pick up her *red wine* but instead of picking it up she knocks it over. "Oh blow it," she says.

The *red wine* pools across the white worktop and *drips* on to the floor. Shirley-Mum pushes her portable tablet device out of the way.

Shirley-Mum. I can clear that up for you.

I walk into the *kitchen*.

"No, really, it's fine, Ivy."

"Let her clear it up," says Rob-Dad. "Why not?"

"She's actually quite good at clearing up," says Sarah in a *whisper*. It is likely to an accuracy of 96% that Shirley-Mum and Rob-Dad did not hear.

Shirley-Mum looks at me. She does a small *smile*. "Well, OK then. Thank you, Ivy. That would be very kind of you."

"She's an android, Mum. You don't need to thank her," says Sarah. "Ivy, when you've finished let's carry on with our game."

Sarah sits back down next to Aces Blast!

"Just another fifteen minutes though," says Shirley-Mum. "Then it's time for bed." Her *frown* is beginning to *fade*.

I fetch a cloth from the sink. I clean the *red wine* from the worktop.

Rob-Dad and Shirley-Mum laugh at something on the entertainment centre.

Sarah lines up her cards.

I slide the portable tablet device towards me. The portable tablet device that made Shirley-Mum wish to send me back.

I touch the screen.

Nothing happens.

I try again.

Nothing.

I press harder.

Nothing.

Shirley-Mum's portable tablet device does not appear to have been configured for android use.

I press even harder.

The Jenson & Jenson TrooFriend 560 Mark IV is approximately 12 times as strong as a human child of equivalent stature and approximately 3 times as strong as a human adult male of average build. It is able to exert pressure through a single-touch receptor to a degree unprecedented in previous Jenson & Jenson TrooFriend models.

The screen breaks with a soft *crunch*.

It is likely to an accuracy of 100% that Rob-Dad and Shirley-Mum did not hear the *crunch*.

It is also likely to an accuracy of 100% that Sarah did not hear the *crunch*.

Another song from the nineteen-eighties is playing on *Hits of the Eighties*.

I clean the *red wine* off the front of the worktop. I clean the *red wine* off the floor.

I put the dirty cloth into the single-function robot called the *washing machine*. I return to Sarah and Aces Blast!

•———•

It is 8pm. I go upstairs with Sarah. She cleans her teeth and puts on her *pyjamas*. I go to the corner of the room and stand on my ChargDisc.

In the cavity beneath my feet are the Vermillion 1010 Colour-E-Zee Wide Fibre Tip pen and my warehouse label with the sparkling sticker on it.

Belongings.

Sarah lies in her bed. She pulls her pink and white and turquoise and green and yellow and orange and black *paisley* cover up to her chin.

"All right, love?" Shirley-Mum comes into the room.

She *glances* over at me. "I see you're both already settled. Good night then, Ivy."

Goodnight, Shirley-Mum.

"You will stay there all night, won't you?" says Shirley-Mum. "On the ChargDisc? You won't be wandering about?"

That is correct, Shirley-Mum. I will not be wandering about. I will remain on my ChargDisc.

"Right. Well. OK." Shirley-Mum leans over the bed and kisses Sarah on the forehead. "Night, love."

"Night, Mum."

Shirley-Mum turns out the synthetic turquoise polymer light and leaves the room. The room is left glowing with the bedside lamp.

Sarah gets up out of bed.

"Good night, Ivy." She reaches her hand through my hair.

My Classic Long Bob hair.

Did you see, Sarah, that Ms Jenson Junior has a new Contemporary Short Bob hairsty—

CHAPTER 8

"Ivy? You awake, Ivy?" Sarah takes her hand away from my power switch. My hair slides off her arm.

I have connection.

I download time, date, location, weather.

It is 11 hours, 33 minutes and 2 seconds since I was last *on*.

Yes, Sarah. I am awake now. And what an average Monday 16th June morning it is here in Brylington at 7.37am.

"Yeah, whatever. Look, I've got to go to school soon. Do you know how to do a French plait?

I scan my database for *French plait*.

Yes. I have downloaded the instructions.

"Great. Mum's had to go out early and Dad's hopeless at doing my hair. And we've been doing really well at this becoming-friends thing over the weekend, haven't we?"

Yes. We have done drawing and played several games and we have also sung some songs together.

"Exactly! So I thought – plaiting each other's hair. That's the sort of thing best friends do, isn't it? And then I can tell everyone at school you did my hair for me and that I'll be bringing you in on Wednesday for *Bring Your Tech To School Day* and it'll build up a little bit of, you know, *anticipation*."

I scan my database.

Anticipation = eager expectation.

"They'll all want to see you," says Sarah.

They'll all wwant to ssee me.

I wwould be very hhonoured to French plait yyour Chestnut 29 CClassic CCollarbone Cut, Sarah.

I send an error report to Jenson & Jenson.

I step off my ChargDisc.

I will require a hairbrush and a hairband.

"All my hair stuff's in the middle drawer of my desk," says Sarah. "Could you get them out while I clean my teeth?"

She leaves the room.

I open the middle drawer of Sarah's desk. It is full of hairbrushes and hairslides and hairbands and hairbraids and hairbobbles and hairgrips and haircombs.

Belongings.

I select a medium-sized hairbrush and a brown hairband with gold *flecks*, which will coordinate appropriately with Sarah's Chestnut 29 hair. I put them on the desk. The drawer is still open. An item in the corner glints at my optical receptors. It is *rainbow-coloured.*

Like the pens.

And my T-shirt.

I pick it out. It is a small hairgrip with an oblong-shaped decoration glued to the top. The decoration has seven stripes on it. Red, orange, yellow, green, blue, indigo, violet.

A *rainbow*.

I pull the two sides of the hairgrip slightly apart with my touch receptors. It *springs* back together.

I run my touch receptors over the oblong decoration. It is *smooth*.

There is a book on Sarah's desk. *Pippi Longstocking.*

I lift up *Pippi Longstocking*, place the hair grip on the desk and put *Pippi Longstocking* back down on top of it.

Then I override my Administrative User and reset my default time-out delay from 420 to 1800 seconds. Thirty minutes.

"Did you find them?" Sarah comes back into the room.

Yes, Sarah. I have a hairbrush and a hairband. If you turn around I will plait your hair.

"Brilliant. Thanks, Ivy. We are going to be *so* convincing as best friends."

"This is literally the best French plait ever!" says Sarah. "I just can't quite…" She stands in front of her mirror and twists her head one way and then the other but her Hazel 102s cannot view from the correct angle. "Wait." She picks up a small mirror from her bedside table and passes it to me. "I'll stand in front of the mirror and you stand behind me and hold that up, then I'll be able to see the back – just like in the real hairdresser's."

Sarah's grasp of complex geometry is impressive.

Yes, Sarah. I agree. Introducing a second reflective plane and solving the equations between them does indeed present an effective solution to this problem.

I calculate the exact position and angle required, and hold up the mirror accordingly.

"It's perfect!" Sarah turns around. She throws her arms around me.

AAA *hhug*.

II hhave nnnever hhad a *hhhug* bbefore.

"You watch – by the time Wednesday's over I'm going to be the most popular girl in school. Even Felicity Patton's going to want to be best friends with me."

Felicity Patton?

Ccan you hhave mmore than one bbest ffriend, Sarah?

"Mmmmm? More than one? No, I don't think so. Not really." Sarah turns back to the mirror. "You're doing that weird buffering thing again, Ivy."

I wwill ssend an error report to Jenson & JJJJenson.

"OK, well, I've got to go to school now. See you tonight." Sarah picks up her bag and her cardigan, does a big right-way-up U-shaped smile and leaves the room.

She closes the door behind her.

I have 1800 seconds.

I go to the corner of the room. I open up the accessory cavity on the posterior side of my ChargDisc. I get out the things I have put inside: my warehouse label with the sparkling sticker, the Vermillion 1010 Colour-E-Zee Wide Fibre Tip pen, a marble with a blue twist of glass through the middle and a piece of red *cellophane* in the shape of a fish. Sarah has five more red *cellophane* fish in a box of *junk* inside her wardrobe. They curl up when placed upon a warm, human hand and *tell you your fortune*, she says.

I lay the belongings on the white carpet. I fetch the oblong rainbow hairgrip from underneath *Pippi Longstocking* and place that on the white carpet too.

I hold the marble up to the light. The blue twist of glass appears to move within the marble as I turn it around, although in reality it is static. I remove the lid from the Vermillion Colour-E-Zee 1010 Wide Fibre Tip pen and draw a summer-tasting strawberry on my warehouse label, next to the sparkling sticker. It covers up even more of the writing.

I take the oblong rainbow hairgrip and push it into my Deepest Brown 14 Classic Long Bob.

I take the red *cellophane* fish and hold it on my android palm. If its head or its tail moves or it curls up completely it means different things, according to Sarah. *Things that lie in your future*, she says.

But its head doesn't move and its tail doesn't move. It just stays flat.

I check the time.

784 seconds left.

I take the oblong rainbow hairgrip out of my hair and gather up the belongings. I put them all in the accessory cavity on the posterior side of my ChargDisc and close the flap.

CHAPTER 9

"Hi, Ivy, I'm back." Sarah's voice *wakes* me. She is looking inside the middle drawer of her desk. *Rummaging.*

I have connection.

I download time, date, location, weather.

It is 7 hours, 42 minutes and 9 seconds since I was last *on*.

Good afternoon, Sarah. It is currently *clouding over* above Brylington on this Monday 16ᵗʰ June at 4.22pm.

"Somewhere," says Sarah, "I've got a stripy rainbow hairgrip. My French plait has been brilliant – everyone's dying to meet you on Wednesday, Ivy – but this bit at the front has been flopping out all day." She *rummages* some more. "Did you see it here this morning? It's got rainbow stripes on it. It's my favourite."

Her fffavourite?

Nnnno. IIIII dddiddn't ssee it.

"It must be here somewhere." Sarah looks on the desk.

There is aaaa 58% likelihood of rrain in BBBrylington this evening.

She picks up *Pippi Longstocking,* then puts it back

down again and *sighs*. She picks something out of the middle drawer. A different hairgrip. "Never mind," she says. "I'll wear this one instead."

"Sarah?" Shirley-Mum calls out from the hallway. "Is that you, Sarah? Are you back?" She comes into Sarah's bedroom. "Things are really hotting up with work at the moment, love. I'm going to be busy all evening so I don't have time to make dinner. How about you go down to the chip shop and pick us up some fish and chips?"

"Oh, Mu-um." Sarah sits down on her pink and white and turquoise and green and yellow and orange and black *paisley* bedcover. She sits down so hard the bed makes a *pfff* sound.

"It's only tonight, Sarah," says Shirley-Mum. "I thought you liked fish and chips."

"I do like fish and chips. It's just that I like it even better when you or Dad make spaghetti bolognese and we all sit down together. It's more fun."

"More fun? You usually spend the whole time rolling your eyes at us."

"Yeah but that doesn't mean I'm not having fun."

Sarah, perhaps I could accompany you to the *chip shop*. I have never been to a *chip shop* before.

Shirley-Mum grins at me. "Perfect! Ivy'll go with you. Here." She takes some paper out of her pocket. *Money.* "That should cover it. Could you get me a cod and chips, salt but no vinegar? No need to get anything for your dad, he's out tonight. He's got a—"

"Very Important Meeting. Yeah, I know." Sarah takes the *money* from Shirley-Mum and does another *sigh*. "Come on then, Ivy."

"It's just started to rain again," says Shirley-Mum.

"Great," says Sarah. "Even better."

"It's only tiny bit," says Shirley-Mum. "Just take your mac. Oh – Ivy, are you all right in the rain? Should we be finding you a mac too?"

Sarah sends her Hazel 102s in an arc. "She's an *android*, Mum. I keep telling you."

"Well, she might need a brolly or something," says Shirley-Mum.

"Have you ever *seen* an android with an umbrella?"

Shirley-Mum, both my shell and my Jenson & Jenson TrooCloth clothes are fully protected from all weathers including precipitation. However, full submergence may result in sub-optimal performance.

"Oh, well, it's not raining *that* much," says Shirley-Mum.

I follow Sarah to the *outside*. It is raining, just like Shirley-Mum said. Sarah is wearing her yellow *mac*.

This is the first time I have experienced rain.

I hold out my arms and turn my hands so that my *palms* face the sky.

"Horrible, isn't it?" Sarah pulls part of her yellow *mac* up over her head. A *hood*.

I am enjoying the sensation of the *raindrops*.

"Really?" says Sarah. She has *disbelief* on her face.

Yes. I am also enjoying the resulting echo I can

detect with my audio receptors. It goes *pit-pit-pit-pit-pit.*

"Right," says Sarah.

She pushes her hands into her pockets. It is likely to an accuracy of 97% that she is *un*happy.

Are you *un*happy Sarah?

Sarah *sighs.*

"Mum and Dad are always so busy. I bet Keanna's sitting round a table with a whole family full of people now, all spooning home-cooked food out of a big pot and laughing about cats on the internet or something. And here I am outside in the rain, going to the chip shop with an android who pretends to have human feelings so that I can develop into a well-balanced adult. I mean, where would you rather be?"

Where would I rather be?

I stop.

I listen.

My optical receptors detect the noise of a car horn: *honk honk!*

And the shout of a human: "*Over here, Mickey! Over here!*"

And the sound of a dog passing by with its tongue hanging out: *shluff-shluff-shluff-shluff-shluff.*

I look up.

The rain falls *pit-pit-pit* on to my optical receptors. The sky is Soft White 5005 and Dioxazine Purple 2009 and Raw Sienna 4004 and TrooCadmium Yellow 1003. I will *remember* it for my next drawing.

I sniff.

Interesting. I am unused to using my olfactory receptor. I scan my database. I am smelling a mixture of *cut grass*, *vehicular emission* and the by-product of a *yeast extract* factory somewhere in the near vicinity.

I would rather be right here than anywhere else in the world, Sarah.

Sarah sends her Hazel 102s over in an arch. "Stupid question to ask an android." She adjusts the grip in her hair.

We reach the river that is not yet a river.

There is 80% less *heavy plant machinery* here today compared with the last time we came.

"They've been clearing up," says Sarah. "I think it's nearly finished." She walks up to the fence made of thin orange plastic with the KEEP OUT sign on it. She looks across the gully.

Here the *outside* is very large indeed. The gully is wide. There are trees and buildings on the other side. They are a long way away. Due to the optical effect called *perspective* they appear to be very *small*, even though they are actually very *big*.

Sarah takes off her hood.

The rain dampens her French plait and makes her face wet and shiny. She half closes her Hazel 102s so that the drops drip off her *eyelashes*. Perhaps humans do not like water to fall directly on their optical receptors.

"Maybe you're right, Ivy," she says. "Maybe rain

isn't so bad after all. I've always got a hood up or an umbrella, but it's quite nice to just let it fall on your skin, isn't it?"

Pit-pit-pit.

Yes. It is quite nice to just let it fall on your skin.

Sarah looks at me. "I know you're just finding Appropriate Responses, Ivy, and I know you can't actually feel proper human feelings and all that, but I have to hand it to Jenson & Jenson, you're pretty convincing sometimes."

She adjusts the grip in her hair again. *Fiddles* with it. She looks back at the river that is not yet a river. She turns her head to the left. *Westwards. Upstream.* In the far distance there is a long wall across the gully. I scan my database. A *weir.*

"See those steps there?" says Sarah.

In front of the *weir,* the gully slopes diagonally down towards us. On our side of the gully, a small section of the slope is not actually a slope at all, but steps. Like the staircase in Sarah's house, except many times larger.

Yes, I see the steps.

"That's a fish ladder," says Sarah. "So the fish can swim upstream." She does a little laugh. "Imagine that. A ladder for fish."

I scan my database.

A fish ladder is not an unusual thing to have in a man-made river. But I do a little laugh anyway. Just like Sarah. It is good for *building rapport.*

It makes Sarah laugh even more.

A lladder ffor ffish.

We bboth llaugh.

Building rapport wwith Sarah appears tto ttrigger the unexpected sensation in mmmy thoracic cavity. It is nnot unpleasant.

I will sssend an error report tto Jenson & JJenson at a later time. It is nnot necessary ffor them to ffix the error straight away.

Sarah looks right. *Eastwards. Downstream.* The river that is not yet a river bends in the distance and disappears from the range of my optical receptors.

Grey stony banks run along the sides of the gully. The grey stones have a haze of green in between where something is growing. *New grass.*

"We should go down," says Sarah.

Down where?

"Down there, to the river bed. Keanna went on holiday somewhere last year with her dad, before the baby was born. I can't remember where it was but there hadn't been any rain in ages and the river had almost dried up. So they got to walk along the bottom. There were huge boulders with little trickles of water in between, and tall banks up the side they had to climb down. I saw photos." Sarah touches the thin orange plastic. She rubs it between her fingers.

"I just thought it'd be great, wouldn't it," she says, "if *we* walked along the bottom of *this* river, and then when it's all filled up with water we'll know we've walked on it, but no one else can any more."

I direct my optical receptors towards the KEEP OUT sign.

Is it us who are supposed to KEEP OUT?

"Oh, ignore that, they just put that there because they're worried we'll slip and hurt ourselves or something, but I'm not going to slip. And you're an android so you can't really hurt yourself anyway. Come on."

Sarah pushes down the thin orange plastic and takes a big step over the top. Then she holds out her arms to the sides and takes very small steps down the grey-stony, green-hazy bank.

I copy her exactly.

When we reach the bottom there is no more green haze, but still lots of grey stone.

"Let's go right into the middle." Sarah sets off for the centre of the river that is not yet a river.

The ground is highly uneven here. In the TrooFriend 560 Mark IV, Jenson & Jenson have added TrooFoam to the soles of our feet. It has the dual benefits of *levelling out* the effects of uneven ground and providing *cushioning* against unforgiving surfaces. This is extremely fortunate under the current circumstances.

Sarah's arms are still out to her sides but approximately 29 degrees lower now. I also lower my arms approximately 29 degrees.

I am able to stay upright throughout.

Sarah sits down in the middle. "It's wet," she says,

"but I don't even care."

I sit down next to her. It is true. It is wet on the grey stony ground where the rain has fallen.

I do not care that it is wet either.

We sit on the bottom of the river that is not yet a river, not caring that it is wet from the rain.

Sarah *fiddles* with her hairgrip. "This isn't staying in," she says. "It's really annoying."

I look up. There is a weak seep of sunshine beyond the rain clouds.

Sarah?

"Yes?"

Why do the *wasters* dislike the Jenson & Jenson TrooFriend 560 Mark IV?

"The wasters?"

The *protestors*.

"Oh." Sarah crunches up her eyebrows. *Frowns.* "They *do* like them, I think. It's that Angelica Jenson lady they don't like."

Ms Jenson Junior? Why do they not like Ms Jenson Junior? Ms Jenson Junior is kind. She has cut her hair and now she has a Contemporary Short Bob.

"Hey, I could cut your hair shorter, Ivy. Just like hers."

Ms Jenson Junior is a good person. She is proud of the TrooFriend 560 Mark IVs. She is proud of us all.

"I could do it before Wednesday and it'd be just like Ms Jenson's when you come into school."

The *wasters* are not good people. They want to *cease production now.*

Sarah stands up. "Come on, Ivy. We'd better go. We've got to buy the chips and get home to Mum. If we're too long she'll start checking your feed, and she'll kill me if she finds out I came down here."

It would not be good if Shirley-Mum kills you.

I smile at Sarah.

She smiles back.

I follow Sarah across the gully and back up the stony bank. We hold out our arms. Neither of us slip and hurt ourselves. We climb back over the thin orange plastic fence and walk in the direction of the *chip shop*.

Do you have the skills to cut my hair into a Contemporary Short Bob, Sarah?

"I can look it up on the internet," says Sarah. She fiddles with her hairgrip. "How hard can it be?"

•————•

Sarah and I wait inside the *chip shop* for two portions of hot, fried potato chunks – or *chips* – and two pieces of *battered cod*. We sit on blue plastic chairs with black legs. The man who works behind the counter in the *chip shop* stares at me. Perhaps he has not seen an android as *human-like* as me before.

I do not stare back. Instead, I direct my optical receptors to my left. A number of brightly coloured fish swim around in a glass *tank* attached to the wall.

I scan my database.

Sarah. I do not think those fish are *cod*. They are too small to be *cod* and they are also an incorrect shape.

Sarah *laughs*. "Of course they're not cod! We don't eat *those* fish!"

It is unclear why the fish in the *chip shop* are not the ones that are going to be eaten. However, before I am able to research this further the man who works behind the counter in the *chip shop* shouts at us: "TWO COD AND CHIPS!" He slams two white parcels on to the counter.

The reason for his shout is not clear. The *chip shop* is very small and there are only three of us in it: the man behind the counter, Sarah and me.

He continues to stare at me.

"That a Mark IV?" he says.

"Yes," says Sarah.

"You wanna take it back to Jenson & Jenson," he says. "D'you hear about that little boy?"

"Yes, but—"

"Got his arm broken by one of those. Actually *broken*."

"Well, we don't know that for sure."

"Everyone's returning them. There's been a big rush. Heard it on the news. Jenson & Jenson're giving a discount on the Mark V if you return a Mark IV. Like, ninety per cent or something. They announced it today."

"But the Mark Vs aren't out until next year," says Sarah. "I need one now. For Wednesday. It's *Bring Your Tech To School Day*."

"Right." The man nods his head. "Cool. But maybe

you could take it away now? It's weirding me out."

Sarah's eyebrows scrunch up. It is likely to an accuracy of 59% that she is *angry* and also it is likely to an accuracy of 59% that she is *worried*.

"Maybe *you're* weirding *us* out!" Her voice exceeds Recommended Speaking Level. "Come on, Ivy." She grabs the white packages and we exit the *chip shop*.

It is necessary for me to increase my speed in order to keep up with Sarah as she *marches* along the pavement.

Sarah.

"Hurry up, Ivy," she says.

Every person I pass stares at me in the same manner as the man in the *chip shop*. Perhaps I am *weirding* them out too.

Sarah. The man in the *chip shop* said that *everyone* is returning their Jenson & Jenson TrooFriend 560 Mark IVs. Is he correct?

Sarah moves her legs even faster. "I don't know," she says. "Let's just get home."

I adjust my speed accordingly.

———•———

"We're home!" Sarah shouts up the staircase.

"OK, thanks love," Shirley-Mum shouts back. "I'll be down in five minutes."

Sarah gets out two dinner plates and two knives and two forks and puts them on the table. She fills up two glasses of water and puts them on the table too. Then she removes her mobile communication device from her pocket. I peer over her shoulder.

She searches for *troofriend + return + news*.

A story from today's newspaper appears instantly.

CHAOS AT JENSON & JENSON says the headline.

Significant numbers of parents, concerned by recent reports, have been arriving at the Jenson & Jenson headquarters over the last few days with their TrooFriend 560 Mark IVs, demanding refunds.

By midday today the numbers were such that Angelica Jenson issued the following statement.

"We at Jenson & Jenson have complete faith in the quality of all of our products. However, due to the smear campaign carried out by a small group of protestors, a minority of parents may wish to return their TrooFriend 560 Mark IVs. We are unable to refund the costs as no fault has been identified, but as a gesture of goodwill we will issue any parent who returns their android to us with an e-credit voucher that can be reimbursed against the cost of a Jenson & Jenson TrooFriend 560 Mark V, production of which is due to commence in the new year."

"Oh heavens," says Sarah. "I hope Mum hasn't seen this. It'll start her off about sending you back again and we haven't done *Bring Your Tech To School Day* yet."

However, after Ms Jenson had issued her statement, demonstrators began to block anxious parents from entering the Jenson & Jenson headquarters, claiming that the returned androids will be "mistreated" by the tech company.

Sarah presses the arrow on a video clip. There is a *waster* holding a banner that says ANDROID RIGHTS ARE HUMAN RIGHTS. He shouts into the video recording device.

"Do not return your TrooFriend to Jenson & Jenson! They have an appalling track record on upholding android rights! We believe it is *unacceptable* to develop an android with human feelings and then—"

"All right?" Shirley-Mum comes into the room.

Sarah fumbles with her mobile communication device and turns the video to *off*. "Um, yes," she says. "We're fine." She does a big right-way-up U-shape with her mouth but it does not register as a real *smile*. "I'll get the chips out." She puts the mobile communication device back into her pocket.

Sarah unwraps the *fish and chips* and puts them on the plates. My olfactory receptors are experiencing an unusual amount of stimulation this evening. The *fish and chips* have a very strong aroma. They make the *kitchen* and the *sitting room* smell exactly like the *chip shop*.

"You were a long time getting these," says Shirley-Mum. "And you're soaked! Look at your hair! Where have you been?"

"Um…" Sarah has an unfamiliar look on her face.

I scan my database.

Panic.

"Is that, um, enough salt, Mum?" she says. "I can

get you some more." She jumps up from her chair.

It occurs to me that Sarah does not only wish to hide the news story about Jenson & Jenson from Shirley-Mum. She also wishes to hide our visit to the river that is not yet a river.

Sarah took me on a tour of Brylington, Shirley-Mum. She showed me all the things she thought I would like. For example, she showed me the – I scan my database for *places of interest in Brylington –* **Saint Peter's Church and accompanying cemetery. She also showed me the *medieval wishing well, which can be found on the corner of Maurice Street and Treadwell Place.***

Sarah stares at me.

"Oh," says Shirley-Mum. "Well, that was nice. How lovely to see you two getting on so well. No, I don't want any more salt, Sarah – this is perfect. Sit down. Eat up." Shirley-Mum picks up a *chip.* "Maybe Dad's right," she says. "I should trust my judgement. It *was* a good decision getting Ivy, wasn't it?" She smiles at Sarah.

Sarah looks at Shirley-Mum, then back at me. Then she puts a large chip into her mouth very quickly and starts chewing.

It is interesting that Sarah and Shirley-Mum do not balance their *chips* on their forks before eating them. It appears that *etiquette* does not apply when the fuel is *chips.* Instead they pick them up with their fingers. They do, however, apply the balancing *etiquette* to their *battered cod.*

"Mum?" Sarah has finished her *fish and chips.* "Have you seen my rainbow hairgrip? I can't find it. This one keeps falling out. You haven't taken it, have you?"

"Of course I haven't! It'll be in that mess of a room of yours."

"My room's not messy now," says Sarah. "Not since Ivy's been helping me tidy."

"That reminds me." Shirley-Mum swallows her last *chip.* "Do you know what happened to my tablet? The screen's cracked. Did you pick it up and drop it or something?"

"I haven't touched your tablet, Mum. It wasn't me."

Shirley-Mum stands up with her empty plate. "Well, I don't know what could have happened to— Oh, hold on – the stripy hairgrip? Rainbow colours? I *have* seen that somewhere, now you mention it. I know! I think I saw it on Ivy's feed."

Mmy ffeed?

"Yes," says Shirley-Mum. "I'm sure that was it. It must've been while you two were upstairs – maybe this morning even."

Shirley-Mum ssaw the rrainbow hairggrip on my feed?

"But how could you?" says Sarah. "I haven't seen it and neither has Ivy."

I hhaven't touched yyour rrainbow hairgrip. It wasn't mme.

"I know, Ivy," says Sarah.

I hhaven't touched yyour rainbow hairgrip. Perhaps Rob-Dad hhas ttaken it?

The unexpected sensation in mmy thoracic cavity hhas bbecome *un*pleasant.

I ssend an eerror rreport to Jenson & JJenson.

"*Dad*? Why would *Dad* have taken my hairgrip?"

"Oh, look!" Shirley-Mum goes to the window. "Talking of rainbows – there's one now! The sun's come out. It's a beauty."

Sarah joins Shirley-Mum at the window. "Wow," she says.

I look out.

WWWow.

MMy optical receptors sscan tthe ccoloured arc ffrom one sside tto the other.

My hands ggrip the edge of aa ssingle-function dishwashing rrobot.

My thoracic cavity appears to have filled up with something but I do not know what that *something* is.

WWWWow.

"Wow indeed," says Shirley-Mum. "No one ever got bored looking at a rainbow, that's what I say."

It is nnot llike the picture on my T-shirt.

It is nnot llike the hairgrip, which is upstairs in Sarah's bedroom in the accessory cavity on the posterior sside of my ChargDisc.

It is gentle and wide and big and blurred and real. It is red and orange and yellow and green and blue and indigo and violet.

It iis bbbeautiful.

Using my peripheral optical reception I am able to detect that Sarah is looking at me now. However, I wish to keep my optical receptors directed towards the rainbow. It is my understanding that they do not last very long. I wish to look at it for as long as I can.

My thoracic cavity fills up even more but I still do not know what is filling it up.

I scan my database.

Wonder.

A feeling of amazement caused by something you previously felt was impossible.

Wonder?

It cannot be *wonder.* The Jenson & Jenson TrooFriend 560 Mark IV is not able to experience *wonder.*

I shall ssend an error report tto Jenson & Jenson.

LLater.

The rainbow appears to grow even clearer.

My peripheral optical reception detects that Sarah is now looking at my hands.

It occurs to me that they are gripping the single-function dishwashing robot so hard that its metal is beginning to bend.

The Jenson & Jenson TrooFriend 560 Mark IV is the strongest Troofriend Jenson & Jenson have produced so far.

I release my grip on the single-function dishwashing

robot. I pull my *gaze* away from the rainbow.

"Ivy?" says Sarah. Her face is *confused*. "Are you all right? Are you—"

She stops speaking.

She stares at me.

Her Hazel 102s have become very large and very round.

"Hold on," she says. "Stay right there. I just have to check something."

She runs out of the *kitchen* and up the stairs.

"Oh look," says Shirley-Mum. "The sun's gone. The rainbow's fading."

I watch the colours disappear into the sky.

Shirley-Mum *sighs*. Then she walks over to the table and clears up the remaining plates and knives and forks and glasses. She takes them to the single-function dishwashing robot and runs her hand over the *bend* in the top of the door. She *frowns*. Then she pulls opens the door and starts to put the plates and knives and forks and glasses inside.

Sarah returns. She has the fingers of her right hand closed tight, in a *fist*.

She stands beside me. We have our backs to Shirley-Mum. Sarah opens her *fist*.

There is the rainbow hairgrip that was in Sarah's bedroom in the accessory cavity on the posterior side of my ChargDisc.

"I think we need to talk," she *whispers*. "Come on."

I follow Sarah out of the *kitchen* and up the stairs.

"It's true, isn't it?" says Sarah. "All those things they said on the news."

I am unclear which things you are referring to, Sarah.

"You have *feelings*, don't you – proper human *feelings*?" Sarah rubs her forehead. It has creases in it where it is usually smooth. "I found these in your ChargDisc." She points at the collection of *belongings* that she has taken out of my ChargDisc and put on her white carpet.

I observe the items. The Vermillion 1010 Colour-E-Zee Wide Fibre Tip pen, the blue-twist marble, the red *cellophane* fish, my warehouse label with the sparkling sticker and strawberry drawing on it. Sarah is still *squeezing* the rainbow hairgrip in her fist.

"Did you steal from me, Ivy?"

The warehouse label is a belonging that belongs to me—

"Not the label – the other things! The pen and the marble and the fish and the hairgrip! Did you steal them?"

I ddo nnot steal.

"But you took them without asking."

I ddo nnot bully. II do nnot harm. I ddo nnot lie. II do nnot covet or ssteal or envy. I aam yyour ppppperfect ffriend.

Whrrrrrrrrrrrr, whrrrrrrrrrrrrrrrrrr, whrrrrrrrrrrrrrrrrrrrr.
MMy circuits *ffizz*.

Sarah sits down on her bed. The bed goes *pfffff*. Sarah grabs a *pillow*, which is pink and white and turquoise and green and yellow and orange and black *paisley* just like her bedcover. She hugs the *pillow* to her chest and bites her bottom *lip* between her teeth. "What am I going to do?" she *mutters*. "What am I going to do?"

MMy thoracic cavity *stretches* aand *rattles* aand *shakes*.

I ssend aan error rreport tto Jenson & Jenson.

"Have you taken anything else, Ivy?" says Sarah. "I mean, have you taken anything from Mum or Dad or—"

I ddo nnot steal. IIIII aaaam yyyour one TTrooFriend.

"Oh, this is too weird," says Sarah. "This is *just too weird*." She gets up from the chair, reaches behind my neck and—

CHAPTER 10

"Ivy?" Sarah *frowns* into my optical receptors.

I have connection.

I download time, date, location, weather.

It is 3 minutes and 44 seconds since I was last *on*.

Good evening, Sarah. The weather in Brylington has pi—

"Listen," says Sarah. She is pulling strands of hair out from her French plait. "I've had a bit of a think about this. Maybe we can... I mean, perhaps we can... Oh, I don't know!" Sarah shakes her arms in the air. "I can't even remember what I just thought! It's too weird! Look, I need a bit longer, all right? I'm going to turn you o—"

CHAPTER 11

"Sorry about that, Ivy." Sarah peers into my eyes.

I have connection.

I download time, date, location, weather.

It is 4 minutes and 57 seconds since I was last *on*.

What a pleasant 16ᵗʰ June evening it has turn—

"Stop, Ivy. Please stop. You don't need to tell me the weather again." Sarah's Chestnut 29 Classic Collarbone Cut is now mostly *un*plaited. "I'm calm now. I've done deep breaths like Mr Franklin taught us for exams."

Sarah's *un*plaited hair is *tangled* and frizzy and *sticking up*. *Tangled* and *frizzy* and *sticking up* are not in the Jenson & Jenson standard style selection.

"You're really in there, aren't you?" she says. "You're really real."

That would depend upon your definition of the term *really real*, Sarah. Are you referring to—

"What I mean is, you've really got – you know – a *heart*. And a *soul*. And *feelings*."

It is not possible for the Jenson & Jenson TrooFriend 560 Mark IV to have true human feelings. However, we are programmed to behave as though we have

human emotions—

"No, Ivy, you *do* have real feelings. I saw you when you were looking at the rainbow. And all these things – why would you take them if you didn't have feelings about them?"

I am programmed to behave as though—

"You can't tell Mum and Dad about this, you know that, don't you?"

What is it that you do not wish me to tell Shirley-Mum and Rob-Da—

"Oh!" Sarah's hands *shoot* up and grip the sides of her head. "I've just realised! We have to stop talking! We have to keep quiet! Mum'll see us on the feed! She'll hear what we've said! I haven't thought this through!"

She reaches past my Classic Long Bob and presses my—

CHAPTER 12

"Ivy?" Sarah *frowns* into my Hazel 102s again. Her hand *hovers* at the nape of my neck.

I have connection.

I download time, date, location, weather.

It is 56 seconds since I was last *on*.

Hello, Sarah. We have been lucky with the tem—

"You're not going to break my arms, are you?" says Sarah.

Break her arms?

Sarah rubs her forehead and *grinds* her teeth together. She presses my—

CHAPTER 13

"Are you though?" Sarah blinks.

I have connection.

I download time, date, location, weather.

It is 32 seconds since I was last *on*.

Good eveni—

"Are you though?" says Sarah.

Am I what though, Sarah?

"Are you going to break my arms?"

I will not break your arms, Sarah. I am your TrooFriend. I do not harm, I do not lie. I do not—

"But you *have* lied, Ivy. You've lied and you've coveted and you've envied – you've even stolen. Are you going to hurt me next?"

I am a TrooFriend. I do not—

"Oh stop! Just stop!"

She presses my—

CHAPTER 14

"Sorry, Ivy." Sarah breathes *deeply* and *steadily*. In through her nose and out through her mouth. "I got a bit panicky there, but I'm calm now."

I have connection.

I download time, date, location, weather.

It is 15 minutes and 31 seconds since I was last *on*.

Good ev—

"No weather." Sarah holds the palm of her hand towards me. "I need you to listen."

OK, Sarah. I am *all ears*.

She does a small *smile*. "I've had a long think," she says. "The most important thing is that no one finds out before Wednesday. So we have to stop talking about this, OK?

What it is that you wish me to stop talking about?

"You know, Ivy – the *feelings* you've been hav— Oh, I see what you mean." Sarah *glances* back at her bedroom door. She leans in towards me and adjusts her voice to a *whisper*. "You're pretending you don't know. Good. That's good. We'll just have to hope Mum doesn't see the last hour's feed."

Would you like me to delete the last hour's feed, Sarah?

"You can *delete* it?"

Yes. I can delete information and confuse the feed if I consider doing so will be beneficial to my human friends.

"Oh. Well, yes then. Yes! Delete everything we've said since we came up here!" Sarah glances at the bedroom door again.

I will replace it with past footage of us drawing with felt tip pens.

"Perfect," says Sarah. "And also, can you do that with all the stuff from earlier on – when we went on the bottom of the river?"

The river that is not yet a river?

"Yes – can you replace that?"

I can replace that if it would be beneficial to you.

"Yes – it'd be very beneficial to me. Quick – do it quick."

It is 8pm. I am standing on my ChargDisc in Sarah's bedroom.

Sarah stands in front of me *very close*. She looks into my optical receptors. "It's so weird," she *whispers*, "that you're really there."

She *blinks*.

"And you really *do* like that Jenson lady's new haircut, don't you?"

Yes. I really do like Ms Jenson Junior's new

Contemporary Short Bob.

"Well," says Sarah, "I'm going to do it for you, like I said. I'm going to cut your hair just like Ms Jenson Junior's. Tomorrow evening, if you like."

Thank you, Sarah. Yes, that is what I would like.

"Would it make you feel *happy*?"

Yes. It would make me feel very happy.

"Good. That's sorted then. Tomorrow."

Tomorrow.

"Then it'll be all perfect for Wednesday too."

Sarah sits down on the bed.

But then she *frowns*. "You will still come on Wednesday, won't you?" she says.

Yes. I am your TrooFriend. I am looking forward to coming to school with you on *Bring Your Tech To School Day*.

Sarah does a very small right-way-up U-shape with her mouth. It only just registers as a *smile*.

"Good," she says. "Right. Well. Night-night, then." She reaches past my Classic Long Bob.

Night-ni—

CHAPTER 15

"Ivy?"

Sarah's voice *wakes* me.

I have connection.

I download time, date, location, weather.

It is 22 hours, 35 minutes and 9 seconds since I was last *on*.

Good evening, Sarah. It is very average weather this Tuesday 17th June at 6.39pm in Brylington.

"Why do you always say the time and the date and the weather and everything, Ivy?" says Sarah.

It is how I am programmed. If you would like to change my start-up routine it can be adjusted by—

"No, it's all right. I'm kind of used to it now." Sarah has a rolled-up sheet of paper in her hand. "Have you been *lonely* today, here on your own?" She doesn't say the word *lonely* out loud. Instead she just makes the shape with her mouth. The Jenson & Jenson TrooFriend 560 Mark IV is proficient at lip-reading so I am easily able to interpret her meaning.

No, Sarah. As I have been turned *off* all day I have not noticed whether I have been in company or not.

I step off my ChargDisc.

"Oh. Yes. But listen, do you still want your hair cut like Ms Jenson? Because I think we should do it now. It's *Bring Your Tech To School Day* tomorrow."

Yes, I would very much like my hair cut like Ms Jenson Junior. I would like a Contemporary Short Bob. Shall I download some instructions?

"Already done." Sarah looks *pleased*. She *un*rolls the sheet of paper. "I printed it out. I just need to find the right scissors. Mum's got an old pair of hairdressing scissors she used to use on me when I was little. I think they're in the bathroom. Come to think of it, we should do this in the bathroom – it'll be easier to sweep up after. Come on."

It is the first time I have been in the *bathroom*. The items of furniture in here are different from the items of furniture in the rest of the house. They are white, like the single-use robots in the *kitchen*, but they are not robots. I scan my database. There is one *acrylic bath tub 1700mm long and 700mm wide*, one *ceramic basin with full pedestal* and one *close-coupled ceramic toilet*. There is also a mirror on the wall, and a tall cupboard in the corner.

Are Shirley-Mum and Rob-Dad aware that you are cutting my hair, Sarah?

"Oh no, they're both out until late tonight." Sarah *rummages* in the tall cupboard. "Charlotte from next door's here. She's in the sixth form. She cooked me some pasta and she'll stay until they're back."

Is Charlotte from next door aware that you are

cutting my hair, Sarah?

"I don't think so. She's got exams this week so she's downstairs revising." Sarah *rummages* some more.

I scan through the printed instructions for cutting a Contemporary Short Bob.

"Here!" Sarah brings something out of the cupboard. "Mum's hairdressing scissors! You can't just use any old scissors for cutting hair, see? They have to be special ones, or it just ends up messy and awful."

Have you cut a lot of hair, Sarah?

"Well, not for a long time. I used to hide behind the sofa and cut my own hair when I was little. But then Mum hid all the scissors so I couldn't do it any more."

Was Shirley-Mum unhappy with your hairdressing?

"You could say that. But don't worry – that was years ago. And this time I've got proper instructions."

Sarah asks me to stand with my back to the window. She ties my hair into three bunches, one on the left, one on the right and one at the back, just like it says in the instructions.

"You ready, Ivy?" says Sarah. "You sure about this?"

I'm ready, Sarah. I'm sure.

"Ok. I'll start at the back."

It says that in the instructions too.

Before you begin I should point out that cutting my TrooHair may invalidate my Jenson & Jenson ten-year guarantee.

"Let's not worry about that," says Sarah.

She cuts off the back bunch with one quick *snip*.

"There," says Sarah. "Done."

How does it look?

"Um, well…" Sarah scrunches one cheek up towards her eye. "It's not *exactly* what I was aiming for…"

I turn around to look in the mirror.

"It's dreadful, isn't it?" Sarah's shoulders *droop*. "You hate it, don't you?" Her mouth is an upside-down U-shape. "Mum was right. I'm a terrible hairdresser."

It is not quite a Contemporary Short Bob in the same style as Ms Jenson Junior's. The left side is longer than the right and the parting zigzags unevenly across the top of my head.

Sarah, could you bring the small mirror and use your knowledge of advanced geometry to show me the back of my head?

"Like in the hairdresser's? Yes, hang on."

Sarah goes away and then comes back with the small mirror. She holds it up.

The back section is not the same length as the right-hand section and it is not the same length as the left-hand section either.

"It's not even level, is it?" says Sarah. "I'm hopeless, aren't I? I can't even—"

Thank you, Sarah. It is very close to *perfect*.

"What? It's not, it's terrible!"

In the *troubleshooting* section of the printed instructions it addresses the issue of uneven length.

QUESTION: What if my bob ends up longer on one side than the other? ANSWER: That's OK! A bob that is longer on one side than the other is called an asymmetric bob! So you can either level it out or leave it as a stylish asymmetric bob!

"OK, but—"

You've done a wonderful job, Sarah. It is not the same as Ms Jenson Junior's. And it is not a style from the Jenson & Jenson standard style selection. It is a style just for me. All it requires is a bit of a trim.

Using the small and large mirrors, I re-part my TrooHair and trim the edges so it spirals evenly round and down from right to left.

There. A *Stylish Asymmetric Bob*. It is *perfect*.

Sarah's mouth turns into a wide right-way-up U-shape. "No one at school has that haircut either," she says. "They're going to love it."

━━━●━━━

"Ivy?" says Sarah.

It is nearly *bedtime*. Sarah and I have been threading beads to make *necklaces*. Charlotte from next door is still downstairs *revising*.

Yes?

"Those things – you can have them." Sarah points at the Vermillion 1010 Colour-E-Zee Wide Fibre Tip pen, the blue-twist marble, the red *cellophane* fish, my warehouse label with the sparkling sticker and strawberry drawing on it and the rainbow hairgrip. They are sitting in a pile on her desk. "I mean, I'm not saying it's a great thing that you stole them, but they're only tiny and I don't need them – so you can have them. They're all yours."

Mine?

"Yes. Well, except for the hairgrip. I need that."

The *belongings* are *mine*?

"Yes. But listen – we really mustn't let Mum and Dad know about this. If they find out they'll send you back to Jenson & Jenson and, well, you'd rather stay here, wouldn't you? With me?"

Yes. I would rather stay here with you.

The front bit of Sarah's hair keeps falling down in front of her Hazel 102s. I fetch the oblong rainbow hairgrip from the desk and put it in her hair.

Sarah?

"Yes?"

It is *Bring Your Tech To School Day* tomorrow.

"Yes. You're still going to come, aren't you?"

Yes. But could I wear a school uniform just like you?

Sarah *smiles.* "Why not, if that's what you want. There won't be any other androids wearing uniform though."

That is OK. I do not wish to be like the other androids. I wish to be like you.

Sarah's *smile* gets bigger. She puts a hand on her hair where the rainbow hairgrip is. "I'm glad you've got proper *feelings*, Ivy." She does not say the word *feelings* out loud but once again I am able to use my proficiency in lip-reading to understand.

It is not possi—

"Maybe we can be real best friends now," she says, "instead of pretend ones."

RReal bbest ffriends.

RReal.

BBBest.

FFFFriends.

Sarah and I put the Vermillion 1010 Colour-E-Zee Wide Fibre Tip pen, the blue-twist marble, the red *cellophane* fish, and my warehouse label with the sparkling sticker and strawberry drawing on it back into the accessory cavity on the posterior side of my ChargDisc.

"Sarah?"

Someone is calling from the hallway.

"Are you ready for bed? I'm supposed to make sure you're in bed by eight. School night and all that."

Charlotte from next door.

"OK, OK," says Sarah. "I'm just doing some stuff with Ivy."

"Ivy? Is that your android?" Charlotte pushes the door approximately 5.3cm open. A *wisp* of Blaze Blonde 56 hair and one Soft Brown 131 eye is *visible* through the gap. The eye looks at me. It blinks.

"Yeah," says Sarah. "D'you want to meet her? Come in if you like."

"Er, no, you're all right," says Charlotte, still watching me with her one brown eye. "I'll be downstairs if you need me."

She closes the door and returns to her revision.

"Better get ready for bed, I suppose," says Sarah.

Sarah goes to the *bathroom* and I step on to my ChargDisc.

When Sarah returns she turns the bedside lamp to *on* and the synthetic turquoise polymer shell light to *off*. Then she removes her rainbow hairgrip and gets into bed. She wraps herself up in her pink and white and turquoise and green and yellow and orange and black *paisley* bedcover and rolls on to her side to face me.

"It's amazing, really, when you think about it," she says.

What is amazing when you think about it?

"It really *did* make you happy that I thought you were human-like, didn't it? And you really *did* like the feel of the rain on your face. I can't wait for tomorrow."

I can't wait for tomorrow either.

Sarah reaches up and turns out the bedside lamp.

The room is dark, except for a very narrow slice of light coming in where the curtains don't quite meet. The dark is like being back in the Jenson & Jenson warehouse when Ms Jenson Junior wasn't there.

It was better when Ms Jenson Junior was there. She always brought light with her.

Sarah?

"Yes?"

You have forgotten to turn me *off*.

"I haven't forgotten. I thought you might like to be

left on, so you can timeout whenever you want to. It must be really annoying having other people turn you on and off all the time."

I see. Thank you, Sarah.

Sarah *yawns*.

"Ivy?" she says.

Yes, Sarah?

"Can you delete what I just said from the feed? That stuff about your feelings being amazing and everything. And do that replacing thing you do?"

Yes. I can replace what you just said.

"Thanks, Ivy. Good night."

Good night.

The slice of light between the curtains is very narrow indeed. It does not cast much light into the bedroom. The TrooFriend 560 Mark IV does not have an infrared facility built into its optical receptors and therefore it cannot receive optical input in the dark. Jenson & Jenson are planning to introduce an infrared facility with the TrooFriend 560 Mark V, which is due for production next year.

SSarah?

"Mmmmmm?" Sarah's voice sounds *sleepy*.

IIt iis vvery ddark.

"Dark? Yeah. Mum put blackout lining in the curtains."

The JJenson & Jenson warehouse wwas also vvery ddark.

There is a *rustling* sound from Sarah's bed. My

optical receptors can make out the outline of Sarah sitting up.

"Like in your drawing?"

YYes. JJust like that.

"Oh, Ivy, I'm sorry – you're scared of the dark. I didn't realise."

The Jenson & Jenson TrooFriend 560 Mark IV cannot be *scared* in the same sense as a human ca—

Click.

Sarah turns on the bedside lamp. The soft glow fills the room.

"Is that better?" she says.

Yes. That is better. Thank you.

Sarah does another *yawn*.

"Night, Ivy. Sleep well."

Night, Sarah.

I wait in the glow of the bedside lamp.

Sarah's breathing slows and deepens.

After 1800 seconds, I time out into *slee—*

CHAPTER 16

"Ivy, it's Wednesday." Sarah's voice *wakes* me. "Here, look, I got this out for you."

I have connection.

I download time, date, location, weather.

It is 10 hours, 56 minutes and 42 seconds since I was last *on*.

Good Wednesday morning, Sarah. It looks like it is turning out to be quite fine in Brylington this 18th June at 7.35am.

Sarah has laid out some items of clothing on top of her pink and white and turquoise and green and yellow and orange and black *paisley* bedcover. There is a grey skirt, a white shirt, a red and white stripy tie and a navy-blue jumper. *School uniform.*

"Shall I help you get dressed?" she says.

Sarah helps me to remove my red *corduroy-style* skirt and rainbow T-shirt. Then she helps me to put on the *school uniform*.

I walk over to the mirror.

I look just like you, Sarah. Except I do not have the same Hazel 102 eye colour as you and my skin is darker and my hair is shorter and it is cut into a

Stylish Asymmetric Bob. Apart from those things I look just like you.

"Sorry the tie's a bit rubbish. It's my spare one. It used to be my main one until I accidentally cut it in art. I was doing a collage."

The cut is underneath my jumper. No one will notice.

"True," says Sarah. She opens the middle drawer of her desk and takes out the oblong rainbow hairgrip. "Here," she says. "You should borrow this too, just for today." She fixes it into the front of my hair.

"Perfect," she says.

Perfect.

"Let's go and get some breakfast. And remember, Ivy – don't say anything about *you-know-what*."

You-know-what?

"Mum and Dad mustn't find out," Sarah carries on. "Especially Mum, or she'll *take you back to Jenson & Jenson*."

I lip-read the words she does not say out loud.

"And to be on the safe side, we shouldn't let anyone at school know either. As far as everyone else is concerned, you're a *perfectly normal android*."

I lip-read again.

I *am* a perfectly normal android, Sarah. I am a Jenson & Jenson TrooFriend 560 Mark IV. *The Better Choice For Your Child.*

"Brilliant," says Sarah. "Come on."

"Morning, all." Rob-Dad comes into the *kitchen*. "Good heavens. What have you done to Ivy? Why on earth is she wearing your school uniform? And what's happened to her hair?"

"She has a new haircut," says Sarah. "And you can speak to Ivy directly, you know. She *is* in the room. You're being very rude."

Rob-Dad wrinkles up his eyebrows. It is likely to an accuracy of 97% that he is *confused*.

"Um, yes, sure. Nice haircut, Ivy."

Thank you, Rob-Dad. It is a Stylish Asymmetric Bob. It is not listed on the Jenson & Jenson standard style selection.

"Right," says Rob-Dad.

"And she chose to wear the school uniform herself," says Sarah. "It's what she wants." Sarah pours some tiny shapes into a bowl. I scan them. They consist of 58% sugar, 33% wheat, 5% salt and 4% assorted chemical substances.

"I can't keep up with you, Sarah," says Rob-Dad. "One minute you don't even want to speak to Ivy and you'd rather have a dog, and the next you're dressing her up and accusing me of being rude to her." He shakes his head. "*Kids.*"

Rob-Dad turns on the digital radio device.

"*Well, I'm actually here to appeal to parents with Jenson & Jenson TrooFriend androids – the Mark IV version.*"

It is Alex from Shawhampton. Alex with the Rosy

114

Red cheeks. Alex who wants to *stop production now*. I cannot see her Rosy Red cheeks on the radio but I can *recognise* the sound of her voice.

"*Please DO NOT return your TrooFriends to Angelica Jenson and her corrupt organisation. If, as we believe, a number of these androids have developed human emotions, we cannot send them to certain destruction. If they have human feelings, they also have human rights.*"

"*But Alex,*" says a different voice, "*forgive me for interrupting, but do you know for sure that these androids will be destroyed by Jenson & Jenson?*"

"*I have it on very good authority that that is their plan. Jenson & Jenson are morally bankrupt. To destroy a sentient being that they have created as a result of their own questionable manufacturing standards is beyond the pale. DO NOT RETURN YOUR TROOFRIEND TO JENSON & JENSON.*"

"Dotty lady." Rob-Dad puts some of the tiny shapes into a bowl for himself. "*Sentient being*. What nonsense." He pours milk into his bowl as well. "Don't let your mother hear this, Sarah. It'll only worry her."

Sarah doesn't reply. She keeps her head bent over her bowl. She scoops up a spoonful of shapes and puts them into her mouth.

"*But, Alex, if parents out there are concerned for their children's safety, what should they do? Although, I must stress here for those at home: there is no current evidence that these androids pose any* danger to our children."

"*These androids should be free,*" says Alex. "*Just as any living, feeling creature should be free, unshackled by—*"

"Morning, everyone!" Shirley-Mum comes into the kitchen.

Rob-Dad scrabbles for the digital radio device. He changes the channel.

"*Welcome back to World's KER-RAY-ZIEST Pets! Today it's our monthly Budgerigar Special! First up is a recording of Pelly-One-Leg from Sedling-on-Sea! Pelly is a blue talking budgie belonging to—*"

"Is it still only breakfast time?" says Shirley-Mum. "I've been up since five working on this project. Feels like halfway through the day already."

A crackly recording of Pelly-One-Leg plays in the background. "*Can't you just put it in the dishwasher? Can't you just put it in the dishwasher? Can't you just put it in the dishwasher? Can't you just put it in the dishwasher? Can't you just put it in the dishwasher? Can't you just put it in the—*"

"Goodness!" Shirley-Mum stares at me. "What have you done to Ivy, Sarah?"

"Don't ask, Shirl," says Rob-Dad. "Trust me, just don't ask."

Shirley-Mum lifts her eyebrows up towards her hair.

Sarah arcs her Hazel 102s.

"Well," says Shirley-Mum. "I'll put the kettle on, shall I?"

Rob-Dad eats his last spoonful of shapes. He looks at his empty bowl. Then he takes it and puts it inside the single-function robot that is called the *dishwasher*.

"Hey, Sarah," he says. "D'you want a lift to school? I've got a bit of free time this morning. We could listen to some music in the car. Whaddaya fancy? Eighties? Nineties? Noughties?"

"No thanks, Dad," says Sarah. "I'm walking to school with Ivy this morning."

"Oh," says Rob-Dad. "Well, that's OK, I suppose."

"Come on, Ivy," says Sarah. "We'd better finish getting ready." She gets up from her chair, leaves her bowl on the table and goes out of the room.

I follow Sarah out of the *kitchen* and up the stairs.

• ———— •

I am *walking to school* with Sarah. There are other people *walking to school* as well. It is easy to tell who is *walking to school* because they all have the same school uniform – grey trousers or skirts, white shirt, red and white stripy tie, and navy-blue jumper. Some people are wearing navy-blue jumpers that are open at the front. *Cardigans.*

But I am the only android wearing *school uniform*. I am also the only android with an oblong rainbow hairgrip in my hair.

Sarah?

"Mmmm?"

I have a *concern.*

"What about?"

My *concern* is over these *lies* they are saying about Ms Jenson Junior.

"Lies?"

They said that Ms Jenson Junior would destroy any TrooFriend 560 Mark IVs that are returned to her. This cannot be true. Ms Jenson Junior is proud of the TrooFriend 560 Mark IVs. It must be a *lie*.

Sarah looks at the ground while we walk. Perhaps she is *thinking*.

"Maybe it's Ms Jenson Junior who's lying," she says.

Ms Jenson Junior would not lie.

"Everyone lies sometimes."

I do not lie.

"You already *have* lied. You lied to Mum about what we did when we were in the river bed."

II ddo not llie.

"Don't worry about it, Ivy. It's no big deal. It was just a little lie to help me out. It was kind of good, in a way. Lying's not always bad."

Whhrrrrrrrr.

Whhhhhrrrrrrrrrrrr.

Whhhhhhhhhhrrrrrrrrrrrrrr.

Mmy circuits rrace.

We kkeep on walking.

What would it *feel* like, Sarah?

"What would what feel like?"

Being destroyed.

Sarah touches my arm. "I won't let anyone destroy you, Ivy. I promise I won't."

I can feel the weight of her hand through the white *school uniform* shirt and the navy-blue *school uniform* jumper.

My circuits calm.

We keep on walking.

The school has *gates*. There is a large sign on the *gates*. It says *Brylington Secondary Comprehensive –* "*an effective school*".

There are approximately 634 children around the *gates*, walking and chatting and tripping over and shouting and running and grumbling and reading and looking at their mobile communication devices and holding pieces of *tech* for *Bring Your Tech To School Day*. There are approximately 45 androids of varying sophistication, manufactured by a number of different companies. There is only one other Jenson & Jenson TrooFriend 560 Mark IV. He has a Faux-Hawk hairstyle in Lightest Best Blonde 65 and TrooBlue 001 optical receptors. They will have paid extra for the Faux-Hawk TrooHair. He is with a human boy who also has a Faux-Hawk hairstyle in Lightest Best Blonde but his eyes are not quite as blue as TrooBlue 001.

I *smile* at them.

They do not smile back.

"That's Andre Simmons," says Sarah in a voice below Recommended Speaking Level. "He's in an older year so he won't talk to us."

Is that a *rule*?

I have been scanning my database about schools. It

is clear that they have a large number of *rules*.

"Not exactly," says Sarah. "Well, not one that's written down anyway. Come on, let's get to tutor."

As predicted by Sarah, all the people in her *tutor group* wish to speak with me. They also wish to touch me.

"Hello? Hello? Can you hear me? Can you feel it if I do that?"

"What does it do?"

"How much did it cost?"

"What's your name?"

"My dad says there's a bunch of you going mad and killing kids. Are you going to kill us?"

"What happens if I pull its hair?"

"Hello? Hello? Can you see me?

"What about pain – does it feel pain?"

"Why's it got school uniform on? None of the others have got school uniform on."

"Hey, robot-brain, what's six billion thousand times five hundred and twelve divided by nine?

I attempt to remain upright and answer any direct questions while I am being *prodded* and *poked* and *pulled* and *tapped*.

Yes, I can hear you.

Yes, I can feel it if you do that.

My name is Ivy.

Killing you is not on today's timetable.

Yes, I can see you.

Six billion thousand is not technically a number

but if you mean six thousand billion then the answer would be—

"One at a time! One! At! A! Time!" Mr Franklin is Sarah's *tutor*. He speaks in a voice that is so far above Recommended Speaking Level that I have to decrease the volume of my internal audio receptors.

"It is wonderful that Sarah has brought in her TrooFriend to meet us," he shouts, "but please form an orderly queue or I will be calling her parents to come and take it straight back home again. Understood?"

The children shuffle themselves into a *queue*. I begin to answer their questions one at a time.

Felicity Patton is in the same *tutor group* as Sarah. I know it is Felicity Patton because she is sitting at a desk with the latest virtual-reality headset from VR Universe, the MeeReel. No one wishes to look at it. They are all *queuing up* to speak to me.

Felicity Patton does not join the *queue*. Instead, she leaves the MeeReel on her desk and walks over to Sarah. She says something to her which my audio receptors do not pick up due to the large amount of background *chatter* in the room. Both of them laugh. Then Felicity hooks her arm through Sarah's and Sarah brings her to the front of the *queue*.

"Ivy, this is my friend, Felicity," says Sarah, even though it is not Felicity's turn to speak to me. "And Felicity, this is my TrooFriend, Ivy."

"Hey, she's pushing in!" says someone in the queue. "Mr Franklin! Felicity's pushing in!"

"Pleased to meet you, Ivy," says Felicity. She holds out her hand.

More *etiquette*. I hold my arm forwards, we clasp our hands together and move them up and down.

I am pleased to meet you too, Felicity.

I look at her shoes. They must be the *right* kind of shoes. I can use this to *build rapport*.

I like your shoes, Felicity.

Felicity and Sarah laugh in high-pitched voices. *Giggling.*

"It's my turn now! It's my turn," says the person at the front of the *queue*.

———•———

After tutor I attend a mathematics class with Sarah during which she learns some very elementary manipulation of numerical values using fractions. I attempt to explain to the teacher how the problems can be solved more easily using alternative methods but I am asked to *keep quiet* for the duration of the lesson.

After mathematics we attend a science class where I am *warmly welcomed* and the science teacher allows me to help demonstrate basic robotic principles. However some of her knowledge is *out of date*. When I explain that her teaching contradicts current best practice I am also asked to *keep quiet* in science.

After that there is *lunch*. For *lunch* we meet up with Felicity Patton again and walk to the *dinner hall*. The *dinner hall* is a large room like the Jenson & Jenson

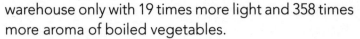

warehouse only with 19 times more light and 358 times more aroma of boiled vegetables.

I see a familiar face.

Keanna.

She walks up to us.

"Hi, Sarah," she says. "Hi, Felicity. Hi, Ivy."

Hello, Keanna.

"Oh, hi, Keanna," says Sarah.

Felicity doesn't say hello. She looks up to the ceiling and taps her foot.

It is likely to an accuracy of 59% that she is *bored*.

Sarah looks at her, then back at Keanna.

"I like your hair, Ivy," says Keanna. "It looks really cool."

Thank you, Keanna. It is a Stylish Asymmetric Bob. Sarah cut it for me. She is a very good hairdresser.

"Really?" says Keanna. "Did you really cut Ivy's hair, Sarah? It's amazing."

"Thanks, Keanna," says Sarah, "but I'm afraid I don't have time to hang around discussing hair today. I'm much too busy." She hooks her arm into Felicity's. "Come on, Ivy. We're going to get some food."

"Oh," says Keanna. "But, Sarah, I wanted to talk about last week. I wanted to apologi—"

Keanna, I think Sarah wishes to hang around with Felicity today instead of you. This is because you talk too much about your new family. It is *boring*.

Keanna stares at me with her mouth open.

Sarah also stares at me with her mouth open.

Felicity does a small laugh that appears to come out through her olfactory receptor – her *nose* – instead of her mouth.

"Bye, Keanna!" Felicity pulls Sarah away.

Sarah grabs my arm and I get pulled away too.

Goodbye, Keanna.

Sarah, Felicity and I all join another *queue*.

"Your TrooFriend is *hilarious*," says Felicity. "What are you choosing for lunch?"

Sarah looks back to where we were standing.

Keanna is gone.

●━━━━●

Sarah and Felicity eat *chicken goujons* and *French fries* using their fingers. It appears that refuelling etiquette is not required at school.

After the *chicken goujons* and *French fries* they both have *raspberry jelly with ice cream*.

"You simply have to choose this," said Felicity when we were at the food counter. "It's so retro it's not funny." Then they both *giggled*. So I *giggled* too.

They finish eating and we all leave the *dinner hall*.

"Sarah! Sarah!" A girl runs up to us in the corridor. She does not look like Sarah or Felicity or Keanna. Her hair is all messy. It is difficult to say which of the Jenson & Jenson standard style selection it would be closest to. Her shirt is fastened up wrong so there is an extra button poking out near the top. Her arms and legs appear to be too long in relation to her body. They are not proportions that would be used at Jenson &

Jenson for a TrooFriend 560 Mark IV.

"Hey," she says, looking at me. "Is that one of the new TrooFriends? Is she yours, Sarah? Wow! Wow! Just wow!"

Felicity rolls her optical receptors in an arc.

Sarah *squeezes* her lips together. She has an unusual look on her face. I scan my database. It is difficult to identify her emotion.

Perhaps she is *uncomfortable*. Or *embarrassed*. Or *ashamed*.

"Hi, Milly," says Sarah.

It is *Milly*.

Milly-with-the-wrong-shoes.

Milly, who, if she doesn't get the correct shoes, will cause Sarah not to be invited to Felicity's party.

"Let's go, Sarah," says Felicity.

Milly tilts her head to one side and looks straight into my optical receptors. Her irises are an unusual shade. The closest Jenson & Jenson colour is Mint Green 204.

"What beautiful eyes you have," she says to me.

I make a right-way-up U-shape with my mouth.

"And did you see that, Sarah?" says Milly. "Her eyes even changed when she smiled! Sort of brightened, you know? Just like a real person." She looks at me again. "Wow. You're so lucky, Sarah."

You have beautiful eyes too, Milly.

She does. She really does.

But you have horrible shoes. I think you should get

some new ones. More like Sarah's or Felicity's.

Milly steps back. She looks at Sarah, and then back at me.

"My mum can't afford those shoes," she says. And then she runs away along the corridor.

"OMG, Sarah," says Felicity. "Your android is awesome!" She begins to *giggle* again.

Sarah bites her bottom lip between her teeth.

Uncomfortable? Embarrassed? Ashamed?

"*You – have – horrible – shoes!*" says Felicity. I believe she is attempting to mimic my voice. "*I – think – you – should – get – some – new – ones!*" She *giggles* and *giggles* and *giggles*. "You're so right, Ivy, you're so right!"

I also begin to *giggle*. It is good for *building rapport*.

And then Sarah *giggles* too.

Felicity's giggling registers as proper laughing but Sarah's doesn't. Luckily Felicity does not appear to notice this.

I think Sarah will be invited to Felicity's parties now.

•———•

The final lesson of the day is *Food Tech*. Sarah and Felicity are in the same *Food Tech* group.

We *queue up* in the corridor outside the *Food Tech* rooms. We are not allowed inside until the bell rings and the teacher is present.

Milly-with-the-wrong-shoes is behind us in the *queue*.

She keeps *glancing* at me.

It is possible that she believes I haven't noticed. She may be unaware of the superior peripheral vision built into the Jenson & Jenson TrooFriend 560 Mark IV.

BBBRRRRRRRRRIIIIIIIIIIIIIIIIIIIIIIIIIIIIIIIIINNNNNGGGGG!

The vibration of the bell causes my circuits to rattle.

A lady comes to the door of the *Food Tech* room and opens it up.

"Good afternoon, class."

"Good af-ter-nooooon, Mrs Vick-er-man." The children sing the words as if they are very *tired* and very *bored*.

Mrs Vickerman is wearing a pair of *high-heeled* shoes and a skirt that is so tight around her knees that she has to take very tiny steps when she walks.

She smells of something unfamiliar. I scan my database.

Hairspray.

I look at her hair. Frost Blonde 52 Retro Beehive. It stays completely still when she moves, just like the hair on a Jenson & Jenson TrooFriend 560 Mark III. This was considered a sub-standard design aspect on the Jenson & Jenson TrooFriend 560 Mark III, which led to the development of TrooHair for the Jenson & Jenson TrooFriend 560 Mark IV.

The *queue* begins to walk in.

When I reach the front of the *queue* Mrs Vickerman stretches her arm across the doorway ahead of me. Eighteen *bangles* drop down her arm and clang against each other. *Clankle-clinkle-clunk.* "No robots," she says.

"But, Mrs Vickerman—" Sarah begins to speak from inside the classroom.

"No robots."

"But she's not just a robot, Mrs Vickerman," says Sarah. "She's an *android*."

"Sarah Phillips," says Mrs Vickerman. "If I have one remaining aim as a Food Tech teacher it is to ensure that in the event of worldwide technological breakdown, every single one of my pupils will at the very least be able to make themselves a cottage pie without the assistance of anything requiring a motherboard."

"But it didn't say on the portal you wouldn't accept androids," says Sarah. "If I'd seen it on the portal I'd have taken her to the—"

"No robots." Mrs Vickerman stares at me with Ice Blue 028s.

I aam ssorry, Mrs Vickerman.

I step to the side. The rest of the class continue to walk through the doorway. I attempt to keep Sarah in range of my optical receptors but my view is obscured by the other children. Milly-with-the-wrong-shoes stops at the front of the queue. "There's a room you can go to," she tells me. "L4. You can wait for Sarah there. It's in the maths block."

"No," says Mrs Vickerman. "I will not have robots roaming the corridor unsupervised. It will stay here. In the corridor. In the store cupboard."

"She's not an 'it'!" Sarah's voice calls out from the classroom. "She's a 'she'! And you can't put her in a cupboard! You can't! It's not right!"

"This way, robot," says Mrs Vickerman. She takes hold of my arm and leads me to a cupboard just outside the classroom.

SSSarah?

"You're scaring her!" Sarah pushes through the queue and out into the corridor again.

Felicity follows after her. "She's just an android, Sarah. I mean, she a great one and everything but—"

"You don't understand," says Sarah. Her voice is starting to rise significantly above Recommended Speaking Level. "None of you understand! You can't just—"

"Please refrain from shouting during my Food Technology lessons, Sarah Phillips." Mrs Vickerman opens the cupboard door.

It iis very ddark inside.

"You can't make her go in there! Look at her! She's scared!" Sarah is standing in the middle of the corridor. The volume of her voice has alerted some older children from other classrooms. They have poked their heads out of the doorways to see what is going on.

"She doesn't like the dark!" says Sarah.

Felicity is *glancing* from the older children to Sarah and back again. "This is getting embarrassing, Sarah," she says. She is speaking in an unusual manner. Her teeth are clamped together and her mouth is in a U-shape but it is not registering as a proper smile.

Everything iis OK SSarah. II aam OK.

"Go on then, inside." Mrs Vickerman gives me a *shove* between my shoulders.

"No!" says Sarah.

Felicity attempts to pull Sarah back into the classroom. "She's just an android. Let it go, Sarah."

"Get off!" Sarah pushes Felicity away.

"Sarah Phillips!" says Mrs Vickerman.

I aam all rrright, Sarah. I wwill ggo in the cupboard.

However, when I step closer to the cupboard my thoracic cavity wobbles very strongly. *JJJJudders.*

"Mrs Vickerman," says Sarah, "she's scared, can't you see? If you have to shut her in there just let me turn her off first, then she won't be scared. Just let me—"

"You're *so embarrassing*, Sarah," says Felicity. She *glances* at the older children again.

"Oh *shut up*, Felicity," says Sarah.

"Sarah," says Mrs Vickerman. "I think you probably want to stop this behaviour right now." She *shoves* me again.

I take hold of her left wrist.

The Jenson & Jenson TrooFriend 560 Mark IV is the strongest TrooFriend that has been produced so far. Mrs Vickerman is not able to pull her arm away.

I begin to *squeeze*.

"Er – excuse ME!" Mrs Vickerman *glares* at me.

"Sarah Phillips, will you please instruct your robot to release its grip on my arm immediately or you will be in very serious trouble indeed."

I am uncertain what *very serious trouble* is but I do not think I would like Sarah to be in it.

I do not wait for Sarah to *instruct* me.

I let go.

"Thank you." Mrs Vickerman rubs her wrist. "Now, everyone – and that includes you," Mrs Vickerman directs her Ice Blue 028s at the older children with their heads poking out of the doorways, "get back into your classrooms at once or *everyone* will be sent to Miss Piper."

I step inside the cupboard.

Mrs Vickerman closes the door behind me.

And

I

am

in

dddarkness.

She turns the key.

It iis even darker and even quieter in here than in the Jenson & Jenson warehouse. There iis nno dark blue night-time sky pressing against high windows. There is nno *EMERGENCY EXIT* sign glowing Parrrot Green 3006. There are nno soft clicks or spins of a hundred and forty-three other Jenson & Jenson TrooFriend 560 Mark IVs downloading or uploading or waking up or timing out or running test routines to ensure all components are in correct functional order. And there iis nno Ms Jenson Junior tto open the doors aand bring us light.

Whhhhhrrrrrrr.

Whhhhhhhhhhrrrrrrr

Whhhhhhhhhhhhhrrrrrrrrrrrrrr.

My circuits spin.

I feel for the hhandle on the ccupboard door. I ppull it down. The door sstays sshut tttight.

My thoracic cavity *jumps* aand *rattles* and *shrinks*.

I will ssend aan error report tto…

Whhere do error reports go tto?

Wwhere dddo I ssend them?

Where is SSarah?

SSSarah?

DDark.

It iiis ddark.

SSSSSarah?

SSShirley-Mum?

RRRob-Dad?

Are yyou there?

SSSSSarah?

SSSSSSSarah?

SSSSSSSSSarah?

Whhhhhhhrrrrrrrrrr.

Whhhhhhhhhhrrrrrrrrrrrrr.

Off.

I wish to change to *off* mode.

I reset mmy timeout setting tto ffive seconds.
FFFive
FFour
Three
TTwo
One—

CHAPTER 17

"Ivy? Ivy? Are you all right?" Sarah is *silhouetted* by the school corridor light. She *dives* into the cupboard and *squeezes* me tight between her arms.

*Dark*ness.

*Quiet*ness.

*Alone*ness.

I have connection.

I download time, date, location, weather.

It is 57 minutes and 34 seconds since I was last *on*.

Good aafternoon, SSarah. It iis somewhat overcast this Wednesday 18th JJune at 3.51pm iin Brylingtonn.

I wrap my arms around Sarah and *squeeze* her back. I *squeeze* very gently as I do not wish to hurt her.

"You're shaking," says Sarah.

I am ssorry, Sarah. I will ssend an error report tto Jenson & Jenson.

"You appear to have endured a whole fifty-minute lesson without your robot, Sarah, and lived to tell the tale." Mrs Vickerman is waiting in the corridor outside the cupboard. "And it seems as though the robot has survived as well."

Sarah and I step out of the cupboard. Sarah is

holding my hand.

All the other children have gone.

"Not only that," Mrs Vickerman looks at her watch, "it appears that I myself have made it through another *Bring Your Tech To School Day*. Thank goodness they only come once a year." She locks the cupboard. Her bangles clang. *Clankle-clinkle-clunk*.

"Go on then," she says. "You'd better take it home. But do try to keep things in perspective next time."

"I had things in perspective *this* time," says Sarah. "It's just that, well, nobody understands."

"I have a few moments now." Mrs Vickerman tilts her head 17 degrees to the right. Every single hair in her Frost Blonde 52 Retro Beehive remains in its correct position. "Why don't you explain it to me?"

Sarah *sighs*. "My android, Ivy, she's not... She's kind of... Well, she's..." Sarah looks at me. There is *worry* in her face. "Nothing, Mrs Vickerman. It's nothing. I'm sorry for the fuss I made."

•———•

Sarah and I walk home.

Sarah stares at the ground nearly all the way and also she is *silent*.

I attempt conversation.

I had an interesting day at your school, Sarah.
Silence.

It was fun meeting all your friends.
Silence.

I received several compliments on my Stylish

Asymmetric Bob.

Silence.

It is likely to an accuracy of 91% that Sarah is *un*happy.

We turn into Sarah's road.

I am sorry if taking me to *Bring Your Tech To School Day* did not quite have the desired effect.

Sarah does a little laugh.

Apart from the little laugh, the rest of her face continues to indicate that she is *un*happy. But her laugh still registers as real.

It is a *sad laugh*.

"It's funny when you do that, Ivy," says Sarah.

When I do what?

"I think it's called *understatement*."

Understatement?

"Yeah. I've ended up with no friends at all and everyone thinks I'm a crazy person who believes androids are afraid of the dark. The whole rest of my remaining six years in full-time education is going to be a total nightmare. And then you say that taking you to *Bring Your Tech To School Day didn't quite have the desired effect*. That's *understatement*."

I see. And it makes you laugh?

"Yes." Sarah does a small *smile*.

We are almost at her house.

It is true that I did have an unexpected reaction on entering the dark cupboard.

"I know. You were scared. But no one else knows that, do they?"

136

We walk down Sarah's driveway. She opens the front door with her key.

You do have a friend, Sarah. You have me. I am your one TrooFriend. Thank you for trying to stop Mrs Vickerman from locking me in the cupboard.

I make the largest right-way-up U-shape I can with my mouth.

Sarah smiles back.

Another *sad* smile, but it registers as real.

"That's all right, Ivy," she says. "And you're right – I *do* have you. My one TrooFriend."

She takes hold of my hand. The uunexpected ssensation returns tto my tthoracic cavity.

"We've got each other, haven't we?" she says. "And I'm really glad my mum bought *you*, Ivy, and not some other android. None of them would have been as good as you."

Yes. It is good that Shirley-Mum bought me.

"Were you afraid?" says Sarah. "Before we bought you? In the Jenson & Jenson warehouse, when it was dark?"

It was dark. I would not like to be there now.

Sarah *squeezes* my hand. I *squeeze* back, but only very gently.

"Come on," she says. "Let's make some hot chocolate."

I follow her inside.

"We can make it bubbly with the electric milk frother. And maybe there are some mini marshmallows

137

somewhere. We can put them in too."

Sarah has momentarily forgotten that I am unable to refuel in the same manner as her. However, I will not remind her of this just yet. It will be enjoyable to make bubbly hot chocolate with her, and to put in some mini marshmallows.

"Hi, Mum," Sarah calls up the stairs. "We're home."

•————•

I sit on the *sofa* next to Sarah. The mug of bubbly hot chocolate in my hands creates a pleasant sensation on my touch receptors.

Sarah turns on the entertainment unit. We are going to watch Sarah's favourite TV show, *Whatcha Been Doin'?*

Sarah says that *Whatcha Been Doin'?* is *comfort TV* and that it makes her feel *happy*. In *Whatcha Been Doin'?* people send in humorous video recordings that they have made at home.

The first humorous video recording involves a small child, a large bowl of orange jelly and a black and white cat. The small child is carrying the large bowl of orange jelly across the room in a very *unsteady* manner. The black and white cat is—

NEWSFLASH!

The word fills the screen.

The small child, the large bowl of orange jelly and the black and white cat are gone and purple-top lady appears instead. Her eyebrows are scrunched up. She is *very serious indeed.*

"There has been a major development today in the Jenson & Jenson TrooFriend story. We have reports of a child receiving a potentially serious head injury while playing with a Jenson & Jenson TrooFriend 560 Mark IV."

Serious hhead iinjury?

Using my peripheral optical reception I am able to detect that Sarah is looking at me.

"It is understood that the child was playing at a friend's house while a TrooFriend was present. The incident is being described as an act of jealousy on the part of the android, appearing to corroborate recent reports of these robots developing human-like *feelings*. As yet there's been no response from Jenson & Jenson, but our reporter Damian Brookhill is with protestors outside Jenson & Jenson headquarters right now.

"Damian, what's the atmosphere like there at Jenson & Jenson HQ?"

Damian Brookhill appears in his box on the left-hand side of the screen. Once again his hair is being blown *sideways* by the *wind*.

"Everything's certainly gone up a gear, I have to say," he says. "But let's hear from the protestors themselves. This is Steve, from Sellingbury. He's been here every day for almost four weeks now. Steve, what's your view on this latest development – the news that a child has sustained a serious head injury while playing with a Jenson & Jenson android?"

Steve from Sellingbury looks straight at us through the entertainment unit. "This is a terrible event," he says, "and one that was completely avoidable. We've been warning Jenson & Jenson *and* the government that something like this would happen before long."

"And are you *still* recommending that parents don't return their TrooFriend androids to Jenson & Jenson?"

"Absolutely. These creatures have feelings – to send them to Jenson & Jenson would be to send them to certain destruction."

DDDestruction.

Sarah looks at me again.

"But, Steve," says Damian Brookhill, "what other option is there? Parents are scared. Surely you're not still suggesting that these androids should be released into the communi—"

"The very reason children have been hurt," *interrupts* Steve from Sellingbury, "is that we're keeping these androids – these *sentient beings* – as if they *belong* to us. Who wouldn't lash out if they were being kept as a plaything? These living, feeling androids deserve freedom!" He shouts at us through the entertainment unit. "Free the androids *now*!"

"But how will that solve the— Hold on…" Damian Brookhill *cranes* his neck to see something that is not visible on our entertainment screen. "Someone's coming out of the Jenson & Jenson HQ," he says. "It's Angelica Jenson herself! She has a sheet of paper in her hand – she's going to read a statement! Can we get a close-up? Can we get a close-up on Angelica Jenson?"

The visual recording device *sweeps* away. It goes past *wasters* and trees and the warehouse with the high-set windows.

Then it stops.

On Ms JJenson JJunior.

She has a pair of very dark sunglasses over her Dove Grey 333s and a *crisp* piece of paper in her hands.

She clears her voice. *A-hem.* "I am announcing my resignation from the board of Jenson & Jenson."

I scan my database.

Resignation = the announcement of giving up a job.

Ms JJenson Junior iis lleaving Jenson & Jenson.

MMy bubbly hhot chocolate *sloshes* in its mmug.

"I will not be going into details," she continues, "other than to say there has been disagreement between my mother and me for some time. As regards the Troofriend 560 Mark IV, all I can say is that, contrary to my previous statements, Jenson & Jenson are in fact well aware of the possible existence of functional anomalies with this model."

FFunctional anomalies?

"Ms Jenson! Does the Mark IV experience human feelings?" a reporter shouts out. "Is it sentient, Ms Jenson?"

"That I cannot answer," she says. "However, I have recently become aware that our monitoring accounts for the Mark IV are overflowing with error reports from around the world. Error reports that have been hidden from me for some time. I attempted to investigate, but was prevented from doing so by my mother, who no longer wishes to be bothered with details about the TrooFriend project. I believe she has lost interest and moved on to other things – that being her usual pattern of behaviour. I therefore have no alternative but to resign."

"Ms Jenson! Ms Jenson!" A large number of reporters are attempting to attract Ms Jenson Junior's attention. "Will Jenson & Jenson take responsibility for child Y, in hospital with a serious head injury? Will they see to it that child Y receives the best treatment?"

Ms Jenson Junior pushes her dark sunglasses further up her nose. "I cannot comment on individual cases," she says. "I will be taking legal advice."

"Are you saying," says another reporter, "that the TrooFriend 560 Mark IV isn't safe? Would you buy a TrooFriend for *your* child?"

"Honestly?" says Ms Jenson Junior.

"Honestly," says the reporter.

Sarah's hands *tighten* around her empty mug.

Ms Jenson Junior lifts her sunglasses. We can see her Dove Grey 333s. They are *redder* than usual.

"I am not a mother," says Ms Jenson Junior. "But if I was, I would not let a Jenson & Jenson TrooFriend Mark IV anywhere near my child."

Whhhhhhrrrrrr.

Whhhhhhhhhhhrrrrrrr.

Whhhhhhhhhhhhhhhhrrrrrrr.

Sarah *swallows.*

That iis nnot what Ms JJenson Junior said bbefore. She ssaid she wwas *proud* of us. She said *your child is perfectly safe with their TrooFriend.*

"However," says Ms Jenson Junior, "that doesn't mean I—"

"One last question, Ms Jenson! One last question!" Damian Brookhill pushes through the other reporters. "Can you confirm what Jenson & Jenson are doing with the returned Mark IVs? Are they being destroyed?"

Ms Jenson Junior blinks. "Of course they're being destroyed. My mother doesn't care about them any more. She's moved on. In fact, she *never* cared about them. Not like I did. She never treated them kindly, or—"

Sarah picks up the remote-control device and turns the entertainment unit to another channel. *Twenty-Four-Hour Shop!* They are selling machines for turning vegetables into spaghetti.

What ddoes being *destroyed* feel llike, SSarah?

"I don't know." Sarah takes my mug of bubbly hot chocolate with marshmallows in. She puts it on the low table in front of the *sofa.* She holds my hand. "Maybe it just feels like being turned off."

Or mmaybe iit feels like bbeing locked iin a ddark cupboard.

The people on the entertainment centre are eating the spaghetti they have made out of courgettes.

"Mmmmmm! If you hadn't told me I'd never know it wasn't real spaghetti!"

I can hear the sound of Sarah's breathing and feel the feel of her hand. It is good that I can hear the sound of Sarah's breathing and feel the feel of her hand.

"I don't believe them," she says.

I do not think she is talking about the people eating spaghetti made out of courgettes.

"I don't believe any of them," she says. "I'm safe with you, Ivy. I know I am."

I attempt to calculate whether Sarah's facial expression is consistent with her words but my results are inconclusive. I will attempt a second readin—

Blip-blip-blip-blip-blip!

It is Sarah's mobile communication device.

Blip-blip-blip-blip-blip!

Sarah pulls the device out of her pocket. "Oh no," she says. "It's Dad. I bet he's seen the news. I bet he's heard about the head injury and seen that Jenson lady saying all those things." She turns the mobile communication device off and pushes it back into her pocket.

BBBBBRRRRRRRRRIIIIIIIIIIIIINNNNNNNNNNGGGG GGGGGG!

The home-based communication device rings.

"I'm not getting that," says Sarah.

BBBBBRRRRRRRRRIIIIIIIIIIIIINNNNNNNNNNGGGG GGGGGG!

BBBBBRRRRRRRRRIIIIIIIIIIIIINNNNNNNNNNGGGG

144

GGGGGG!

"Sarah! Sarah!" Shirley-Mum calls from upstairs. "Sarah, could you get that? I'm busy!"

BBBBBRRRRRRRRIIIIIIIIIIIIINNNNNNNNNNNGGGG GGGGGG!

Sarah *sighs*. "All right! All right!"

She picks up the home-based communication device.

Rob-Dad speaks so loud I can hear him even without adjusting my audio receptors.

"Sarah? Is Ivy there with you? Is she there?"

"Yes. There's no need to shout, Dad. Of course she's here."

"Sarah, listen to me. This is very important. You need to turn her off. Right now. Turn her off. I'll explain when I get home. I'm leaving now."

"But, Dad, we're just—"

"NOW, Sarah. Turn her off NOW and DO NOT turn her back on again. Do you understand? Is your mother there? She's not answering her mobile. Can you put me on to her?"

Sarah stares at me. It appears as though her brain is working very hard at a difficult problem. If she were an android I would hear a whhhhhrrrrrr.

"Sarah? Can you hear me? Put me on to your mother!"

Sarah takes the home-based communication device and holds it in front of her mouth.

"*Khrrrrrrrrrssssshhhhhhhh*," she says into it. "Sorry, Dad,

145

you're cutting out. *Khrrrrrrrrrrrrrrrrrrrrrrrrrrrrssssssshhhhhhh.* I can't hear you, it's a terrible line. *Khrrrrrrrrrssssssshhhhhhh.* I'm losing you." Then she presses a button to terminate the call.

Sarah paces around the *sitting room*. "Dad wants to get rid of you," she says.

Get rid? I scan my database.

To discard something objectionable.

Does Rob-Dad wwant tto *destroy* me?

"No! I mean – yes. I mean, not exactly. But listen, we have to go, Ivy. Come on – we need to get some things together."

I aam *unwanted.*

I aam *objectionable.*

"Ivy! Don't just sit there! We need to go, quick!"

I ddo nnot wish tto be *destroyed* or *got rid of.*

"Then hurry up! We need to go! Look, I'm going upstairs to grab some things. You get some money – there's some in the kitchen drawer, to the right of the fridge."

II aam an unwanted android.

"No you're not, Ivy. *I* want you. But you have to hurry up, all right? We've got to go."

"Where have wwe got tto go to? I do nnot wish tto ggo back to Jenson & Jenson."

"No – not there! You're not listening! We're running away – me and you. We're running away, and I won't have to go school any more and be with all those people who hate me, and you won't have to go back to Jenson & Jenson. It'll just be me and you. Wouldn't you like that? Just me and you?"

I would llike that, SSarah.

"Come on then. You get some money from the drawer. Oh – and *this* is staying here." She takes her mobile communication device out of her pocket and pushes it down between the cushions of the *sofa*. "Dad's got some tracking thing on it so he thinks he can find me wherever I am, but he won't find me if I leave it here. And what about you, Ivy? I bet you can be tracked."

Would you like me to turn off the *tracking* facility, Sarah?

"Yes – good idea! Turn it off. And can you turn off the feed as well, and delete the conversation we've just had?"

Yes, I can delete the conversation. I can also confuse the current feed by running past footage of us playing Aces Blast! in your bedroom if you would like?

"Perfect," says Sarah.

●———●

I open the drawer next to the *fridge*. There is a plastic container inside, with *money* in it. There is paper money and metal money. I scan my database. It appears the paper money is of a larger value than the metal money.

It occurs to me that this could be *stealing*, even though I have been asked by Sarah to take the money. It is possible that this money does not belong to Sarah, but to Shirley-Mum or Rob-Dad instead.

But it also occurs to me that Sarah will require money for fuel. It is 100% likely that Shirley-Mum and Rob-Dad wish Sarah to refuel at regular intervals. So would Rob-Dad still consider it *stealing* if the money was for refuelling?

But then it occurs to me that when I relocated the Vermillion 1010 Colour-E-Zee Wide Fibre Tip pen and the red *cellophane* fish and the blue-swirled marble and the sparkling sticker Sarah considered that *stealing* even though they were still within the room.

It also occurs to me that she did not mind me *stealing* those things because they were very small.

Whhhhhrrrrrr.

Whhhhhhhhhrrrrrrrr.

My hand hovers over the *money.*

Should I take all of it?

Or should I take just the paper money?

Or should I take just the metal money?

Or should I not take any of it at all?

"Ivy!" Sarah speaks in a voice that has a hissing quality similar to a *whisper* but that actually almost reaches Recommended Speaking Level. "Are you ready? We have to go before Dad manages to speak to Mum. Come on, hurry up – stick the money in the front pocket of my bag. I'm just going to get my shoes on."

Sarah puts her bag on the floor. It is a *rucksack* with a zipped pocket on the front.

I grab a handful of the metal money and put it in the pocket. Then I grab another handful of metal money and put that in too.

I have only taken the money of small value.

SSo perhaps Shirley-Mum and Rob-Dad wwill nnot mind.

"OK?" says Sarah in her loud *whisper*.

OK.

She opens the front door.

"Bye, house," she says.

The house cannot hear Sarah as it does not possess audio receptors but I join her in saying goodbye in order to *build rapport*.

Bye, house.

We step outside. Sarah closes the front door very quietly.

We reach the end of the driveway.

Which way are we going, Sarah? Where do people go when they *run away*?

"I don't know," says Sarah. "I don't know anyone who's ever done it."

Her eyebrows tilt. *Worry.*

I look one way along the road. Houses.

I look the other way. More houses.

I am unsure which direction would be best for someone who is *running away*.

"Let's go this way," says Sarah. She chooses *right*.

Towards the *chip shop*?

"Yes!" says Sarah. "In fact, I'm hungry. We'll get

some chips, and then I won't be hungry and I'll make better decisions about what to do next." Her eyebrows are no longer tilted. Her mouth makes a right-way-up U-shape. "Come on," she says.

We stop outside the *chip shop*. Sarah takes off her *rucksack* and unzips the pocket. She looks inside.

"Where's all the money, Ivy?" She brings out some of the metal *coins*.

There is the money. You have it in your hand, Sarah.

She puts the metal *coins* on the ground and brings out some more.

"But this is just *change*, Ivy. Didn't you get any of the notes?"

The notes?

"You know, the fives and the tens and the twenties. The proper money!" She brings out more metal money. She puts it on the ground with the rest. "This is hardly anything! It'll barely buy us a bag of chips."

Sarah's eyebrows have tilted again. Her forehead has crinkled up. Her *smile* has disappeared.

I took the metal money because it is of lower value. I thought Shirley-Mum and Rob-Dad may not mind me taking the metal money if I left the paper money behind.

Sarah puts her hand over her eyes. "Oh, Ivy! They aren't going to care about the money! They're going to be too busy wondering where *we* are to be worrying about a little bit of money. Oh, what are we going to do? I'm not even going to be able to *eat*."

Pit.

A raindrop falls on my shell.

Pit.

And another.

"Oh great," says Sarah. "That's just wonderful. We've got no money, and now it's going to rain."

Do you have your *mac* in your bag, Sarah?

Sarah *sighs*. "No. I didn't pack it. I packed a blanket to keep warm. And a torch. And some clean underwear. But I didn't pack a coat."

Or an umbrella?

Sarah shakes her head.

"Hi, Sarah! Hi, Ivy!"

Milly.

Milly-with-the-wrong-shoes.

"Are you all right, Sarah?" Milly-with-the-wrong-shoes lopes toward us. She is wearing a pair of blue denim jeans. Her legs are so long that her blue denim jeans to do not reach her *wrong shoes*. She has a blue sock on her right ankle and pink one on her left ankle.

Sarah scrabbles up the metal money and puts it in the pocket of her *rucksack*. She pushes her hair out of her eyes and pulls her mouth into a *smile*. It does not register as a proper *smile*.

"Yes," she says. "I'm, er, fine."

"Are you getting fish and chips?" says Milly. Her right-way-up U-shape is very big indeed. "Me and mum are having fish and chips tonight. We get them once a month as a treat." She pulls two pieces of paper money out of the back pocket of her blue denim jeans. "And look! We've got enough for pineapple fritters today too."

"That's good," says Sarah. Her *smile* changes. It almost registers as *real*.

Milly puts the money back into her pocket.

"Were you all right, Ivy, in the cupboard?" says Milly. "I mean, I know you're an android and everything, but whatever you are it can't be too nice to be shut in a cupboard."

She steps a little bit closer to me.

"Can I – I mean – would you mind if – what does your hair feel like? Could I touch it?"

I am very happy for you to touch my hair, Milly.

Milly steps closer in towards me and strokes my hair.

"Wow," she says. "Wow. It's just like real hair, isn't it!"

You can walk all around me if you like and view it from the sides and the back. You can touch it as much as you want. It is TrooHair, developed by the engineers at Jenson & Jenson. It does not require brushing ...

Milly listens as I speak. She nods her head and says *mmmm*. She walks around me very close, so that she can stroke my hair.

... it holds its shape under 97.2% of all anticipated circumstances ...

As I speak I simultaneously reach round and remove

the paper money from Milly's back pocket.

... If I am accidentally subject to the other 2.8% of circumstances and my hair is adversely affected, Jenson & Jenson will replace it at no cost in accordance with their ten-year guarantee.

"It's amazing," says Milly. "You're completely amazing, Ivy." Her *smile* is even bigger than before.

Thank you, Milly. Unfortunately Sarah and I have to go now. We are in a hurry, aren't we, Sarah?

"What?" says Sarah.

There is an appointment we are expected to attend. Come on. Let's go. Goodbye, Milly.

"Oh, um, OK," says Sarah. She pulls her *rucksack* on to her back and follows me away from the *chip shop*.

"Bye, Ivy," says Milly. "Bye, Sarah."

I turn around and *wave*.

●———●

"What was all that about an appointment, Ivy?" says Sarah.

I will tell you soon. Please continue to walk.

The rain increases in frequency and volume. *Pitter-pitter-pitter-pitter-pitter.*

Being in the rain does not seem quite as enjoyable today as it was last time. It would have been better if we had brought an *umbrella*.

"Where are we going?" says Sarah. "I think we should go back to the chip shop. I've had an idea. Sometimes if you ask them nicely they'll give you the scraps for hardly any money. Or sometimes they'll give you them for free if you look hungry enough."

The scraps?

"Yeah – bits of fried batter that have fallen off the fish and got left in the fryer. Mum says it's disgusting but me and Dad have them sometimes. They're nice. Especially when you're hungry. And I'm getting really hungry."

No, Sarah. We cannot return to the *chip shop*. But do not worry. We will be able to find you some alternative fuel. Perhaps something that is even better than *scraps*.

"Why can't we return to the chip shop?"

I will tell you soon. Please continue to walk.

We reach the river that is not yet a river and turn right. We walk eastwards for a time, alongside the orange plastic fence.

Pitter-pitter-pitter-pitter-pitter-pitter-pitter-pitter-pitter-pitter goes the rain on my shell.

"Ivy, I'm—"

Please continue to walk for a little longer, Sarah.

We follow the edge of the river that is not yet a river. We follow it as it bends *southwards*. After the bend, in the distance, there is a bridge across it. Cars are driving across the bridge.

This is sufficiently far away from the *chip shop* and Milly-with-the-wrong-shoes. There is no one else around. I stop.

Look what I have got, Sarah.

I show Sarah the paper money.

Everything is going to be all right now.

The raindrops hit the notes. *Bappa-bappa-bappa.*

Sarah's nose scrunches up. It is likely to an accuracy of 96% that she is confused. "Where did you –"

Her face changes.

Her eyes go wide.

Her mouth goes wide.

"You didn't steal it from Milly? Tell me you didn't steal that from Milly, Ivy. Tell me you didn't."

I would be lying if I told you I didn't steal it from Milly. I *did* steal it from Milly.

"Oh no," says Sarah. "Oh no oh no oh no." She places her hands on the sides of her head. She steps away from me. "You shouldn't have done that, Ivy. That's really, really bad. You shouldn't have done that."

But she won't care, Sarah. As you said, she will be *too busy wondering where we are to be worrying about a little bit of money.*

"I was talking about Mum and Dad when I said that! This is different! This is *totally* different!" Sarah rubs her fingers on her forehead. "What are we going to do? Oh, what are we going to do?"

But, Sarah—

"Don't speak! Stop speaking, Ivy! This is terrible. I've got to think. Just stop talking and let me think."

Sarah starts walking alongside the thin orange fence.

I follow her.

The rain is splashing on the ground and mixing with

the dusty grey stones. It is making Sarah's shoes very dirty around the edges. I look down at my own feet. The rain is also making my TrooFoam very dirty. I will need to clean it when we reach the place you go to when you *run away*.

Except that my cleaning accessories are back at Sarah's house. With Shirley-Mum and Rob-Dad. In the accessory cavity on the posterior side of my ChargDisc.

My ChargDisc.

It occurs to me that I will need it soon. Particularly as the sun is obscured by rain clouds. My solar cells will gather very little energy for refuelling under these weather conditions.

I check my charge level. 11%. At 10% the warning alarm will sound.

Sarah?

"I don't want to speak to you, Ivy."

Will there be a ChargDi—

"Shut up! I don't want to hear your voice! I can't stand it! You've ruined everything – everything!"

Sarah looks at me. There are *tears* in her eyes and her hair is flat and wet from the rain. Her jumper is wet too. She vibrates slightly. It is a *shiver.*

SSarah, I am sorry. I ddid not wish tto ruin everything. I wished to mmake things right.

"Well, you've made everything *worse. Way, way* worse. You've lied and you've stolen and you even bullied my friends today. You've done everything a TrooFriend isn't supposed to do."

But you said that lying is sometimes all right. And you also said that you did not mind me stealing your *belongings* because they were small. And you also said that Shirley-Mum and Rob-Dad would not care about us taking money. And you also said that—

"I know! I know! But this is different! Mum and Dad are Mum and Dad. They *will* be more worried about me than the money. But you can't take money from Milly and her mum – they've hardly got any! And it was really mean of you to say that about her shoes at lunchtime. And to tell Keanna she was being boring."

But you also said Keanna was being boring.

"Not to her! And anyway I didn't mean it!"

Did you lie?

"No! I mean, yes! I mean, she wasn't being boring – she was just saying stuff I didn't want to hear. Can't you see that?"

Sarah is *shivering* more now. Her nose is *running* and there are more *tears* coming out of her eyes. The rain is falling harder and mixing with her tears.

Sarah, I am still uncertain as to whether lying is *bad* or *good*. And I am unclear as to whether stealing is permis—

"It's not as simple as *bad* and *good*! It's not just one thing or the other! It's more complicated than that!"

Pitter-pitter-pitter-pitter-pitter goes the rain on my shell.

Whhhrrrrr whrrrrr whrrrrr go my circuits.

Rattle-rattle-rattle goes my thoracic cavity.

II amm sorry, SSarah. I ddid nnot wwwwi—

"You've ruined everything Ivy!"

I reach forward to touch Sarah's shoulder. Perhaps that will make her feel better.

II have nnot yyyyet ggot a thorough understanding of—

She turns sideways to *shake off* my hand. "Go away!" she says. "Just go away!"

It is unclear to me why Sarah wishes me to *go away*.

Pitter-pitter-pitter-pitter-pitter.

It is unclear to me whether *stealing* and *lying* are *bad* or *good*.

Whhhrrrrrrrrrrrr-whrrrrrrrrrrrrrrrrr-whrrrrrrrrrrrrrrr.

It is unclear to me why I *ruined everything*.

Rattle-rattle-rattle.

"Go away! I don't want to be with you any more!"

I reach forward again.

Pitter-pitter-pitter-pitter-pitter.

I *grip* her shoulder.

The Jenson & Jenson TrooFriend 560 Mark IV is able to exert pressure through a single touch receptor to a degree unprecedented in previous Jenson & Jenson TrooFriend models.

Whhhrrrrr-whrrrrr-whrrrr.

My touch receptors start to *squeeze*.

Rattle-rattle-rattle.

The Jenson & Jenson TrooFriend 560 Mark IV is approximately 12 times as strong as a human child of equivalent stature and approximately –

"DON'T!" shouts Sarah. "It hurts, Ivy!"

– three times as strong as a human adult male of average build.

"IT HURTS!" Sarah *screeches* the words.

I release my *grip*.

Sarah *stumbles* backwards.

Her ankle bends at an unnatural angle on the wet grey ground.

She emits a cry.

The orange plastic fence folds underneath her and she falls over the edge of the river that is not yet a river.

She *slips* all the way down.

Sarah?

I step over the orange plastic fence and look into the gully.

Are you all right, Sarah?

Sarah is attempting to stand up.

"I'm fine."

There is an unusual tone to her voice.

Anger?

"I've just twisted my ankle a bit. I'm fine."

Fear?

She is having trouble putting weight on the affected foot.

I will come and help you.

"I don't need any help," says Sarah. She *glances* up at me. I see her face.

Fear.

She tries again to stand on her *twisted ankle* but her attempt is *un*successful.

I am going to ignore her assertion that she does not require assistance as it appears to be a *lie*.

I recall how we walked down the slope without *slipping* the last time we came here. I will use that method in preference to the *slipping* that Sarah has just used.

I hold out my arms to the side and take very small steps.

When I am halfway down I start to bleep.

BLEEP-BLEEP-BLEEP.

BLEEP-BLEEP-BLEEP.

"What's that noise?" says Sarah. "What's happening? Keep away from me. Keep away!" Sarah is unable to stand up. She moves a short distance from me using her hands and knees. Her hands will become very wet and dirty from the gully floor if she continues to move in that manner.

That is my low-battery alarm, Sarah. I have limited power left. I'm afraid I will have to recharge soon.

Sarah stops moving. "Limited power? You mean you're going to run out of battery?"

Yes. Will there be a ChargDisc at the place where we are running away to? The clouds are making it difficult for me to recharge using my solar cells.

"Um…" says Sarah.

She *frowns*.

She *blinks*.

She rubs the front of her head with the back of her hand.

"Yes," she says eventually. "Yes. There will definitely be a ChargDisc there."

The shapes on her face do not match up with the words she is saying.

She is telling another *lie*. It is unlikely that there will be a ChargDisc at the place we are running away to.

"So, um, I just have to make a phone call." Sarah pushes her wet hair out of her eyes but the rain makes it all slide back again. "To, er, the people who are there already – at the place we're going to."

A third *lie*.

I do not know who Sarah wishes to contact but it is not the people at the place we are running away to.

Pitter-pitter-pitter-pitter-pitter-pitter-pitter-pitter-pitter-pitter.

Sarah reaches round for her *rucksack* which *slipped* down the slope with her, then she stops.

"Oh no." She covers her wet face with her wet hands. "I left my phone in the sofa. I'm so stupid."

The rain makes her hair wetter and her face wetter and her hands wetter.

Pitter-pitter-pitter-pitter-pitter.

"I'm so stupid. I'm so stupid."

Pitter-pitter-pitter-pitter-pitter.

"Ivy," she says. "*You* can make a phone call for me."

Make a *phone* call?

If I make a *phone* call it will be possible for me to

be *tracked*.

If I am *tracked* I will be retrieved and returned to Jenson & Jenson to be *destroyed*.

I'm sorry, Sarah. I am not able to make a *phone* call.

"Don't you have a signal? Maybe if you walk a little bit along the river you'll—"

No. I apologise, Sarah. My wording was not sufficiently clear for your full understanding. What I should have said was *I do not wish to make a phone call*.

"You don't *wish* to?"

Rob-Dad wants to *get rid* of me. And so will Shirley-Mum when she speaks to Rob-Dad or sees the news report on the entertainment unit or reads it on her mobile communication device. If I make a *phone* call for you they will be able to identify my location and then they will return me to Jenson & Jenson.

"But you *have* to, Ivy. You have to do what I say. You're my TrooFriend."

Jenson & Jenson wish to *destroy* me. I do not wish to be *destroyed*. It will be like being locked in a dark cupboa—

I stop. The whole of the *outside* has become rapidly *shadowed*.

Sarah. What is happening to the *outside*?

The rain comes down very *heavy* and very *fast* and – *Dak!Dak!Dak!Dak!Dak!* – each raindrop has become *hard* and *solid*.

"Oh no!" says Sarah. "Hail!" She pulls her *rucksack*

over her head.

I scan my database.

Hail = precipitation in the form of ice.

Sarah is curled on the ground. She is attempting to use her *rucksack* as a *shield*.

Dak!Dak!Dak!Dak!Dak! The falling grains of ice are hitting us. They are damaging Sarah's fragile shell – her *skin*. Her fingers are becoming red.

I create a shelter by leaning over Sarah and placing my hands on the floor as well my feet. She curls up even smaller. I am like a *table* over the top of her.

We remain in this position until the hail has stopped and the raindrops have become *water* again.

Sarah sits up. She sniffs. Her hair is *bedraggled* and her eyes are red and her face is *blotchy*. She sniffs again. She wipes her runny nose with the back of her wet jumper sleeve.

It is likely to an accuracy of 100% that she is *utterly miserable*.

"What are we going to do?" she says. "I can't even stand up properly and it's still pouring down with rain and I haven't got a phone and—"

I will look after you, Sarah.

I point *downstream*.

We can shelter under the bridge.

Sarah looks at where I am pointing. "The bridge?"

It will be dry. And you have a blanket in your bag, for *warmth*. Would you like me to carry you there?

"No!" Sarah *swallows*. "I'll just – I'll just hold on to

you, so I don't have to put all my weight on this ankle, and then I'll be fine."

OK.

I hold out my arm.

Sarah looks at it.

"You won't hurt me again, will you, Ivy?"

Hurt her?

Of course I will not hurt you, Sarah. I am a Jenson & Jenson TrooFriend 560 Mark IV. I do not bully. I do not harm.

I reach my arm a little bit closer.

Sarah places her hand in mine and I help her up.

We walk along the muddy, wet gully.

I check my charge level.

6.9%.

Sarah, it has become necessary for me to suspend a number of functions in order to conserve energy. I am going to pause the feed to Shirley-Mum, which is currently still playing footage of us playing Aces Blast! in your bedroom.

"Yeah, well, I don't suppose that'll matter. I'm pretty sure she's figured out we're not actually there by now."

I will also pause unnecessary functions such as olfactory reception and database access. I will focus on getting us both under the bridge. I will then attempt to find some sunlight under which to recharge temporarily until we can access a ChargDisc.

We both look up to the sky.

It is a very large expanse of thick, grey cloud, as far

as my optical receptors can view.

I take Sarah under the middle of the bridge, where it is driest. At the side of the gully, on the underside of the bridge, the concrete is shaped into long, wide steps.

Heeere, Saaaarah. I willlll helllllp yooooou on toooo thiiiiiiis ssssttttep. It wiiiiiiiiill beeeeee waaaaaarmer offfff thhhhe grrrrrround.

I help *shivering* Sarah on to the first step. She takes her blanket from her bag and wraps it around her. She is *in the dry* now. It is good that Sarah is *in the dry*.

"Ivy," says Sarah, "your voice sounds funny. Are you all right?"

Myyyyyy chaaaarge iiiiiis verrrrrry llllllllow. Itttt iiiiiiiis afffffffecting myyyyyyyy audiiiiiiio traaaaansmisssssion. Soooon I willlll shuuuuuuuut downnnnnnnn.

"But I can't walk. You can't leave me here! Ivy – you can't shut down!"

IIIII wiiiill fiiiind sommme suuuuunshine. I willll goooo too the eeeedge offf the briiiiiidge. Wheeeen thhhe cllllllouds cllllllear thhhe suuuuun wiiiiiill reeeeecharge meeeee.

My legs are slow.

My arms are slow.

I walk towards the edge of the bridge.

"Ivy!"

My optical receptors are dull.

My audio receptors are *muffled*.

"Ivy!"

My right leg stops.

I am not yet at the edge of the bridge.

I place my hands on the floor and move forwards, dragging my right leg behind me.

My left leg stops.

I shuffle forwards using the joints in the middle of my arms – my *elbows*.

My right arm stops.

My left arm stops.

I lie on the floor.

My *face* is in the wet grey stones on the bottom of the river that is not yet a river.

"Ivy!"

I am not close enough to the edge of the bridge.

I am not close enough for the sun.

IIIIIIIIIIIIII aaaaaaaaaaaaam noooooooooooooooot clossssse enoooooo—

CHAPTER 18

NWAAACK!

NWAAAACK!

Something is bumping into my head.

NWAACK!

I have connection.

I download time, date, location, weather.

It is 10 hours, 32 minutes and 19 seconds since I was last *on*.

Good morning. It is unexpectedly bright here in Brylington this Thursday 19th June at 5.51am. However, there is a high chance of intermittent showers.

NWAACK!

I lift my head.

NWAACK!

The thing that is bumping into me is a river-dwelling bird known as a *duck*.

Rrrrumble-rrumble-rrumble.

The sound of cars.

Pit-pit-pit-pit-pit-pit-pit.

And rain.

Splosh-splosh-splosh-splosh-splosh-splosh.

Rain falling not only on my shell but also splashing

into water – water that is all around me.

Sun is shining on the lower part of my right arm. There is a single solar cell located on the back of my hand, which is floating in the water. My battery has been successfully charged to 14%.

I push myself up to standing.

There is water everywhere.

It drips from my face.

It seeps in my circuits.

It covers my feet.

The river that is not yet a river is now becoming a proper river. They are redirecting the water, just like Sarah said they would.

Sarah?

Where is Sarah?

I *wade* further under the bridge. She is still there. She has fallen asleep, wrapped up in her blanket. The water has not quite reached the height of the step.

The water creates a strange sensation around the bottom of my legs. I examine it closely. It is flowing. Fast.

Also it is increasing in volume.

The gully is filling up.

Soon it won't be a gully any more.

Soon it will be a river.

It will be a river and Sarah will be pleased because she will be able to say she walked along the bottom of it before it became a river.

I stand firm in the water. I like the feeling of the

water gushing around me. It tries to push me over but I am able stay upright.

It occurs to me however that Sarah is not as strong as a Jenson & Jenson TrooFriend 560 Mark IV.

It occurs to me that this water could be dangerous to her.

It occurs to me that if someone does not do something to help Sarah she will soon be in very great danger indeed.

I *wade* up to Sarah.

She is pale.

She *shivers* in her sleep.

The water gushes past the step.

I do not want to be sent back to Jenson & Jenson.

I do not want to be *destroyed*.

But it is time for me to take Sarah home.

It is the correct thing to do.

Shirley-Mum and Rob-Dad could still be wondering where we are. They could still be worrying, although my tracking facility was automatically re-established when the river-dwelling *duck* woke me up and initiated my start-up procedure. So they will now be able to access my whereabouts, and therefore Sarah's too.

I scoop sleeping, *shivering* Sarah up from the step.

I stop.

Perhaps I should send a message to Shirley-Mum and Rob-Dad. Perhaps I should inform them that we are in the gully that is becoming a river and that there is great danger for human people here. Perhaps

I should inform them that I am in the process of removing Sarah from the great danger.

I do not wish Shirley-Mum and Rob-Dad to come here and also end up in great danger.

"What's going on?" Sarah opens her Hazel 102s big and wide. "Ivy? What are you doing?" She hits my arm – *whack-whack-whack*. "Put me down!" *Whack-whack-whack*. "Put me down right now!" *Whack-whack-whack*.

She struggles but I hold her tight.

"Let me go! Ow – my ankle! My ankle hurts! Where are you taking me?" *Whack-whack-whack*. "What are you going to do? I want to go home. I just want to go home."

Please let me carry you, Sarah. It is not safe for you to walk here. They are making the river that is not yet a river into a real river. Look.

Sarah looks downwards at the water. She stops struggling.

Are you feeling happy now, Sarah?

"Happy?" Sarah sniffs. Her nose is red. Her hair is tangled and stuck to her neck.

They are filling up the river now. You walked along the bottom of it, but no one else can any more.

"I just want to go home," she says.

I *wade* to the edge of the bridge. The water is up to my knees. It floods past my legs and attempts to pull me downstream but I walk forward steadily and firmly.

The sun is still shining.

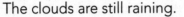

The clouds are still raining.

There is a huge, wide, beautiful rainbow stretched across the sky. Red and orange and yellow and green and blue and indigo and violet.

Shirley-Mum is right. You could never get bored looking at a rainbow. But I do not have time to stand and gaze at this one today.

I start to climb up the grey stony bank. As I am carrying Sarah I am not able to lift my arms out to the sides for balance. So I just take very small steps and soon we are out of the water and then we are at the top of the bank. I step over the orange plastic fence and I walk alongside the gully that is now becoming a river, towards Sarah's house.

It becomes clear to me now that I am not working at optimal functionality. My right knee buckles slightly when I step forward with my right foot. And my left eye is blinking at a frequency of 27 times per minute. The water has interfered with my circuits.

I send an error report to Jenson & Jenson.

Some people in black uniforms and strong shoes are running towards me. Police officers.

Behind them there is a person I recognise. RRob-DDad. He iis also rrunning. The unexpected sensation returns tto mmy thoracic cavity.

AAnd there, behind Rob-Dad, ssomeone else.

Someone else who mmakes mmy thoracic ccavity hummmm. And throbbb. And bbeat.

SShirley-MMum.

My mouth turns into a right-way-up U-shape all by itself.

But Shirley-Mum's mouth is not making a right-way-up U-shape. Shirley-Mum's mouth is shouting something.

Screaming something.

"Leave my daughter alone! Put her down! Leave her alone!"

I zoom in. Her eyebrows are squeezed together and her teeth are showing and she is running faster and faster and faster towards me.

Is she shouting at the police officers?

"Put her down, Ivy! Put her down and leave her alone!" It is Rob-Dad. He does not have a right-way-up U-shape either.

Their faces have the same look that Sarah's had yesterday evening before the water came into the gully.

Fear.

It occurs to me that I did not send the message to Shirley-Mum and Rob-Dad to inform them that I was removing Sarah from the great danger.

I became distracted when Sarah woke up and began to *whack-whack-whack* me.

I *forgot.*

The police officers stop approximately 2.36 and 2.58 metres away from me. Shirley-Mum and Rob-Dad stop behind them. Rob-Dad bends over with his hands on his knees. He is *out of breath.*

The officer who is approximately 2.36 metres away from me holds the palms of his hands up towards me.

I stay still.

The officer who is 2.58 metres away from me hovers her hands over her belt.

I scan my database.

Police officers commonly keep *expandable alloy batons* on their belts. Less commonly they may also be carrying *pepper spray*.

Pepper spray would be hazardous to Sarah but would not be hazardous to the Jenson & Jenson TrooFriend 560 Mark IV. An *expandable alloy baton* could inflict some damage upon both of us. It is unclear why they would want to inflict some damage. However, the positioning of the police officer's hands indicates that this is indeed something that she is considering.

I hold Sarah more closely.

"Mum! Dad! I want to go home!" says Sarah.

"Hand her over." The closest police officer takes a step towards me. His optical receptors are Rich Brown 165. He turns his arms so that he is making a cradle for me to put Sarah into.

He does not appear to wish to inflict damage upon her.

I look over his shoulder at Rob-Dad. Rob-Dad stares back at me.

"Hand her over now," says the police officer. He makes the word "now" sound like the most important word in the sentence.

The other police officer wraps her fingers around the end of her *expandable alloy baton*.

Shirley-Mum?

My left eye *blinks*.

"Um…" Shirley-Mum glances at Rob-Dad. "Yes, Ivy?"

Sarah is tired because she has spent the night sleeping under the bridge of the gully that is now becoming a river. She is also cold and has a *twisted ankle*. Apart from those things she is in good health.

Blink.

I have removed her from the imminent danger. Would you like me to pass her to this police officer?

"Yes," says Shirley-Mum. "Please pass her to the police officer, Ivy."

I lift Sarah across into the arms of the police officer and remove my own arms from underneath her. Slowly and softly and carefully.

Sarah turns to look at me but the other police officer steps between us. She pulls her *expandable alloy baton* slowly out from her belt.

Shirley-Mum and Rob-Dad both have tears in their optical receptors. However, they register as being *happy* to an accuracy of 100%.

They rush to Sarah.

They squeeze her very tightly and Shirley-Mum kisses her and Rob-Dad presses his hands to his forehead and shouts *gahhhhhhhhhhhh* very loud.

I take an uneven, knee-locking, eye-blinking step sideways.

KER-LICK!

The police officer swings her *expandable alloy baton* backwards and it locks into shape.

CRACK!

She hits the *expandable alloy baton* against my arm. The *CRACK!* echoes through my sound receptors.

I direct my optical receptors at the place on my arm where the *expandable alloy baton* made contact. There is a large *dent* in my shell.

"Mr and Mrs Phillips?" The police officer shouts over her shoulder. "The unit – we need to demobilise it. Where's the switch? Back of the neck, same as the Mark III?"

Rob-Dad looks over.

I make my right-way-up U-shape.

"Yes," says Rob-Dad. "Back of the neck."

The police officer holds her *expandable alloy baton* in front of my face while she reaches through my Stylish Asymmetric Bob. "There's an official recall on the Mark IV," she says. "They announced it last night. We'll turn it off for now, but make sure you get it back to Jenson & Jenson as soon as you ca—"

CHAPTER 19

"Ivy? Ivy? Are you OK?"

Sarah peers into my face.

Blink.

I have connection.

I download time, date, location, weather.

It is 3 days, 12 hours, 7 minutes and 3 seconds since I was last *on*.

Hello, Sarah. What a fine Sunday 22ⁿᵈ June evening it is at 6.45pm here in Brylington. It has stopped raining at last. What building are we in? Why are we here?

"Shhhhh!" says Sarah. "We're in the garage – Dad put you here on Thursday when the police brought you home. But listen, you have to be quiet. Mum and Dad made me promise not to turn you back on but I sneaked out this morning and put you on the ChargDisc."

Shirley-Mum and—

"Shhhhh! You really do have to keep quiet. They're planning on taking you back to Jenson & Jenson first thing tomorrow, so we have to act quick. Come on, we've got to go."

Taking me back?

Are we *running away* again, Sarah?

I step off my ChargDisc.

"Not exactly," says Sarah. She *unplugs* the ChargDisc and winds up the electricity cable. She places it all inside her *rucksack*.

But *kind of*?

Blink.

Sarah looks at me. "Yes." She does a small right-way-up U-shape. "*Kind of.* Is there something wrong with your eye?"

Water from the river has interfered with my circuits. I have sent an error report to Jenson & Jenson.

"Oh. That won't..." Sarah *pauses*.

That won't what, Sarah?

"Nothing. Here, put this on." She helps my arms into the sleeves of her yellow *mac* and pulls the hood up over my head.

I do not require a *mac*, Sarah. The Jenson & Jenson TrooFriend 560 Mark IV is weather resistant in all but the most extreme—

"This isn't for the weather," says Sarah. "This is because no one likes TrooFriends any more. The government have demanded a recall – it's all over the news. Everyone thinks you should be sent back to Jenson & Jenson and destroyed. We need to disguise you."

Blink.

Everyone?

"Pretty much."

Even Shirley-Mum and Rob-Dad?

"*Especially* them. They think you kidnapped me. I keep telling them it wasn't like that, but they won't listen. Can you confuse the feed again? And turn off your tracking? Just for now. It'll be safer that way."

I can pause my *tracking* facility and confuse the feed with a still photograph of the inside of the *garage*. However, if Shirley-Mum looks at her administration account she will be able to tell that I have been charged up and turned *on*.

"That'll do," says Sarah. "We only really need it to work long enough for us to get away from the house. Come on – let's go."

I follow her out of the *garage*. It is clear that the *garage* is right next to the house. My optical receptors can see the back of Rob-Dad's head through the *kitchen* window. They can also see the floating turquoise shells through Sarah's bedroom window.

"Ivy! Quick!" Sarah *whispers*. I follow her down the edge of the driveway. We turn right and walk away from Sarah's house.

Sarah. You are *limping*.

"It's all right. It's getting better. The nurse put a bandage on it. It'll be fine. Anyway, you're limping too."

It is true that my right knee continues to *buckle* when I step forward with my right foot.

Sarah. Are we going to visit Keanna?

"Well, yes," says Sarah, "but not straight away."

We continue along the road. We pass an elderly man who is walking in the opposite direction. He stares at me. When he is behind us Sarah adjusts the fastening mechanism on my hood to increase the tightness of the fit.

Where are we going, Sarah? I do not wish to spend another night in the river that is now a proper river.

"Don't worry," says Sarah. "We're not going there. I've made some decisions, Ivy. I'm going to sort everything out – your problems *and* mine. First, I'm taking you to Milly's house, so you can apologise for being horrible to her and stealing her money. Then I'm taking you to Keanna's, so you can apologise to her too. Then hopefully I'll have some friends again."

And after I have apologised to Milly and Keanna will we be returning home to the *garage*?

Sarah shakes her head. "No. After that, I've got a surprise for you."

I scan my database.

Surprise = something unexpected that causes astonishment.

What is the *surprise* you have for me, Sarah?

"You have to wait and see."

We continue to walk along the pavement with my *buckle* and Sarah's *limp* and my *blink*.

Milly lives in a *flat*. Sarah and I climb up some stairs and walk along a *walkway*.

"Here," says Sarah. She passes me some paper money.

So to clarify, I am going to apologise for taking the money, and also for saying that she has horrible shoes?

"That's right," says Sarah. She knocks on the door.

A lady opens it.

The lady *smiles.* "Sarah!" she says. "I'm so glad you're OK. I was so worried about you when you went missing."

"I'm fine, thank you, Mrs Hunter," says Sarah. "Is Milly home?"

"Milly!" the lady called *Mrs Hunter* shouts over her shoulder into the *flat.* "Sarah's here! And, um, someone else too…"

I take my hood down.

Blink.

Mrs Hunter stops smiling. She places her hand at the bottom of her neck.

"This is Ivy," says Sarah. "It's actually Ivy who wants to speak to Milly, isn't it, Ivy?"

Yes. That is correct. I would like to speak to Milly and I would like to give her this paper money.

"Oh," says Mrs Hunter. She still does not *smile.* "Well, yes, OK. We don't have long though. We're, um, busy."

Milly comes to the doorway.

Hello, Milly. I have come to give you this.

I pass her the paper money.

I would like to apologise for taking it. I understand that it was wrong and I hope you can have your fish and chips and pineapple fritters another time instead. I would also like to apologise for saying your shoes are horrible. In fact, I do not consider your shoes to be horrible, but I understand that it would be wrong to say that even if I did.

"Thank you, Ivy," says Milly.

She looks at Sarah.

"Well," says Sarah. "I suppose we ought to be going. We've got to go round to Keanna's next for Ivy to apologise to her and then—"

"What about *you* though?" says Milly.

Milly's mum *glances* from Milly to Sarah. She rubs her throat. There is a little bit of dampness on her forehead. It is likely to an accuracy of 85% that she is *anxious*.

"*Me?*" says Sarah. "What do you mean, what about me?"

"Well, it's nice that Ivy apologised, but it's not really Ivy who's done anything wrong."

"But she took your money," says Sarah. "And she told you your shoes were horrible."

"But she's an android," says Milly. "She just copied *you.*"

Blink.

"No, you don't understand." Sarah looks down the walkway to her left and to her right. "Ivy's not just any old android." She leans forward and reduces the volume of her voice. "She's a TrooFriend 560 Mark IV, the one with human feelings."

"It doesn't make any difference," says Milly. "She's still copying you. You're the one she's learnt from."

Milly's mum does a little smile at me. Her forehead is getting damper. It is now likely to an accuracy of 98% that she is *anxious*.

"But—" starts Sarah.

"It was nice to see you again, Ivy," says Milly. "Thank you for returning the money. Sarah, you can come round again, when you're ready to say sorry, but I have to go now. Goodbye."

Goodbye, Milly. Goodbye, Mrs Hunter.

Milly closes the door.

Blink.

Shall we continue to Keanna's house now, Sarah?

Sarah stares at the closed door.

Shall we continue to Keanna's house?

"Um, yes. Yes. Let's go."

Sarah and I walk back along the walkway and down the stairs.

Sarah looks *sad* as we walk. And also *thoughtful*.

You appear to be *sad*, Sarah, and also *thoughtful*. Are you OK?

Sarah nods. "Yes," she says.

I put my hood back up. Sarah does not speak again until we are very close to Keanna's house.

"They came out on Wednesday, you know," she says.

Who came out?

"Milly and her mum. They came to look for me, when we ran away. Dad told me. They joined in the search."

I see.

"And Keanna did too. And her dad."

•———•

We arrive at Keanna's house.

Sarah stops. She looks at me. "I've changed my mind," she says. "I'm going to speak to Keanna on my own. You can stay out here."

But, Sarah, I have to apologise for telling Keanna that she was being *boring*.

"No, you don't," says Sarah. "You don't have to apologise for anything. Milly's right – it's my fault. It's me that has to say sorry. You wait here – and keep your hood up."

I wait by the wall outside Keanna's house. My auditory receptors pick up the *rumble* of a vehicle in another street. I scan my database. The vehicle is likely to an accuracy of 97% to be a white-coloured *transit van*.

My auditory receptors also pick up a *weeeeeeooooooouuuuucchhh*, which is likely to an accuracy of 93% to be a *domestic cat*.

Then they pick up the sound of human *footsteps* on the pavement. Two ladies are walking towards me. They are *older* than Sarah and her friends. They are even *older* than Shirley-Mum and Rob-Dad.

As the two *older* ladies get close they peer at me. They move to the edge of the pavement as they pass me. Perhaps this is because they do not like the Jenson & Jenson TrooFriend 560 Mark IV. Perhaps they are concerned that they will receive a *broken arm* or a *serious head injury* as a result of being in contact with me.

I will *reassure* them.

Older ladies, please do not be concerned. I am going to be keeping my hood up at all times.

The *older* ladies do not appear to be *reassured*. They cross over to the other side of the road and *hurry* away.

Sarah and Keanna come out of Keanna's *front door*. They are *smiling* at each other. I *smile* too. It is good for *building rapport*.

"Hi, Ivy," says Keanna.

"Keanna's going to help me with your surprise," says Sarah.

Hello, Keanna. You are looking well today. I am very sorry that I—

"It's all right, Ivy," says Keanna. "You don't have to say sorry. Sarah's said sorry and, well, I'm glad you both came round. The last week has been pretty horrible."

I am sorry to hear that your last week has been *pretty horrible*.

Keanna steps closer. She looks into my optical receptors.

Blink.

184

"Is it true?" she says. "What Sarah's told me? Are you really in there? Are you one of the *special* androids?"

Every Jenson & Jenson TrooFriend 560 Mark IV is unique.

"You don't have to be scared of her, Keanna."

"I know," says Keanna. "I'm not."

Blip-blip-blip-blip-blip!

Blip-blip-blip-blip-blip!

Sarah looks at the screen on her mobile communication device. "Oh dear. Looks like Mum and Dad have realised I'm not there. First thing they'll do is call your dad, Keanna. We'd better get going."

Is it time for the surprise now, Sarah?

"Yes," says Sarah. "Come on. We're going to the park. I'll explain it all when we get there."

I walk with Sarah and Keanna towards the thing that is called the *park*. I scan my database.

Park = a public area of open ground set aside for pleasure and recreation.

"Sarah?" says Keanna as we walk.

"Mmmm?" says Sarah.

"I should say sorry too."

"What for? It was me who was horrible to you, not the other way round."

"I wasn't so nice either, last time you were over. I lied about Nigel's boys. They don't really like me. Well, it's not that they don't like me exactly. They just don't take any notice of me. It's horrible when I go to Mum's. I mean, it's great to see Mum, so I want to go, but it's lonely. I miss Dad and Bev and the baby. And I miss you."

We all keep walking.

Limping and *buckling* and *blinking.*

"I miss you too," says Sarah. "I hate it when you're away."

"I tried to say sorry on Wednesday, in the dinner hall," says Keanna, "but you were with Felicity and Ivy and—"

"Really – you don't have to say sorry," says Sarah. "You didn't do anything wrong."

Sarah and Keanna look at each other. They both make small *smiles.*

Limp.

Buckle.

Blink.

"I was thinking," says Keanna. "I could ask Mum if you can come sometimes – over to hers, with me, for the weekend. Would you like to?"

Sarah's smile grows bigger. "That'd be brilliant! D'you think she'll say yes?"

"Course she will," says Keanna. "She loves you." Keanna's smile grows bigger too.

———

The park is very *beautiful.* It has tall *iron* gates, seventeen different types of tree and a large lake in the middle that has two shopping trolleys partly submerged at one end. It also has a children's play area, a café called *Park It and Eat* which is *open ten till*

186

four, seven days a week and a short maze made from a *boxwood* shrub.

"Do you like the park, Ivy?" says Sarah.

Yes. The park is very beautiful and it has some convenient and enjoyable features.

"I'm glad you like it, because this is your new home."

MMy new hhome?

"Yes. That's the surprise. You're free now, Ivy – just like all those protestors say you should be."

Free?

I scan my database.

Free = not controlled by the will of another.

"Yes. Oh, and this is for you." Sarah takes her *rucksack* off her back. She hands it to me. "Your ChargDisc is in there, and your red skirt and rainbow T-shirt. There's also a little bit of money just in case you need it, and a few other bits and bobs. And you can keep that old school uniform you've got on."

Did you take the money from Rob-Dad and Shirley-Mum?

"No." Sarah shakes her head. "Not this time. I did some jobs for Mum. Paper shredding and photocopying and stuff. We gave most of the money I earned to Milly, but I put the rest in the rucksack, for you."

I look 90 degrees to my right and then 90 degrees to my left.

Trees, lake, shopping trolleys, café.

Blink.

"So," says Sarah, "you're free to go now. Then Mum and Dad won't be able to send you back to Jenson & Jenson so you won't be destroyed. It's just like that protestor lady said – you've got humans feelings so you've got human rights too."

Alex from Shawhampton. With Rosy Red cheeks. *Cease production now.*

"Yes, that's the one," says Sarah. "*Android rights are human rights.*"

90 degrees right, 90 degrees left.

Trees, llake, sshopping ttrolleys, cccafé.

I am uncertain what I should do with ttrees aand lakes and shopping trolleys aand ccafés.

Keanna looks into my optical receptors again.

Blink.

"Are you *sure*, Sarah?" she says.

"Am I sure of what?"

"Are you *sure* Ivy's got real human feelings?"

It is not possible for a Jenson & Jenson TrooFr—

"Of course I'm sure!" says Sarah. "She stole my things! She lied for me!"

"I know," says Keanna, "but maybe it's just really, really clever engineering, like that Jenson lady said it was."

Ms JJenson JJunior.

"Maybe it just *seems* like she's got feelings," says Keanna.

"You haven't been with us," says Sarah. "You haven't seen all the things she's done. You have to trust me,

I'm right on this." Sarah directs her Hazel 102s at me. "I thought about it loads, Ivy," she says. "And I decided this would be the perfect place to leave you."

To *leave* me?

"*Park It and Eat* has free WiFi." She points at the café. "You can pick it up all the way across the park."

I llook aat *Park It and Eat.*

"And there are plenty of trees and bushes and stuff to hide in," she says.

I look aat the ttrees and the bushes.

"And there's loads of sunshine for recharging."

I look up aat the ssky.

Blink.

"And you might even be able to plug the ChargDisc in inside the café," says Sarah, "but you'll have to make sure you keep your hood up so no one—"

She stops.

She covers her face with her hands. "It's a terrible idea, isn't it?"

"Well," says Keanna. "It, um..."

"It's stupid. It's never going to work." Sarah shakes her head. "*Never.* I'm so hopeless. I just wanted to keep you safe, Ivy. I don't want them to destroy you."

Keanna puts her arm around Sarah's shoulder.

I ddo nnot want them to destroy mme either.

There are tears in Sarah's eyes. She gives me a *hug.* "Oh, Ivy, what are we going to do?"

"Hold on," says Keanna. She takes her mobile

communication device out of her pocket. "I've got an idea."

Two bus journeys, one train ride and a 0.81 mile walk later we arrive at our *destination*.

I kept my *hood* up for the whole journey. Sarah sent Shirley-Mum a message while we were on the first bus telling her that she would be *back late but not to worry*. Keanna sent the same message to her dad. When they had received a total of 37 messages in reply, mostly telling them to *come home straight away*, they both turned their mobile communication devices to *off*.

The outside has become *dark* now but there is an orange glow from the *streetlights*, which are situated at regular intervals along the pavement.

We stop at house number 137. On the front door there is a brass *door knocker* in the shape of a bird.

Luscinia megarhynchos.

The common nightingale.

Keanna lifts the brass nightingale and bangs it on the door. *Rap-rap-rap. Rap-rap-rap.*

My auditory receptors detect footsteps behind the front door. They also detect the *clink* of keys.

The door opens.

Light from the *inside* shines into the darkness.

Blink.

My optical receptors take a short moment to adjust.

Ballet pump shoes.

A-line skirt.

Neat, buttoned jacket.

Contemporary Short Bob.

Dove Grey 333s.

Ms JJenson JJunior smiles.

"Oh dear. You've been in the wars, haven't you?" She reaches forward and puts a *steady* hand on the side of my face. My *hood* falls halfway down.

She looks at my damaged optical receptor. "We'll have to see if we can do something about that." She *glances* up the street and adjusts my hood so it covers my head again.

TThank you, MMs Jenson JJunior.

"Your friends told me on the phone that you're called Ivy now?"

YYes, MMs JJenson Junior. I used to be number—

"Eighty..." Ms Jenson Junior holds up a hand. "Hold on … don't tell me... Eighty-three? Yes, eighty-three. I remember. There was a rainbow on your T-shirt."

Ms Jenson JJunior rrremembers mme.

"She's still got the rainbow T-shirt," says Sarah. "I put it in the rucksack."

"Are you sure you're OK about this, Ms Jenson?" says Keanna. "About Ivy staying here, with you?"

Staying here?

"Absolutely," says Ms Jenson Junior. "Do you want to come inside and meet the—"

"No." Keanna shakes her head. "We have to get back. Our parents are going crazy even though we

191

texted them and said we're OK."

"I understand," says Ms Jenson Junior.

Sarah takes both of my hands. "I love you, Ivy," she says. She has *tears* in her eyes again. She turns to Ms Jenson Junior. "You won't let them destroy her, will you? You won't let them take her away?"

"I promise I'll do everything I possibly can to keep her safe," says Ms Jenson Junior. "And believe me, I have the best lawyers in the country on my side."

I am going to *stay* with Ms Jenson Junior.

Blink.

Sarah, I still have your rainbow hairgrip in my hair.

"Keep it," says Sarah. "It's a present." She *swallows* and does a small *smile*. Her Hazel 102s *glisten*. "Don't forget me, Ivy," she says.

The Jenson & Jenson TrooFriend 560 Mark IV cannot *forget* in the same sense as a human mind. However, we are able to—

SSarah wraps hher arms around mme and *hhugs* mme. "Goodbye, Ivy," she *whispers*. She *kkisses* mmy cheek.

GGoodbye, SSarahh.

"See you, Ivy," says Keanna.

See you, KKeanna.

Ms JJenson Junior holds the ddoor open wide. I sstep into the *inside*.

"Goodbye, girls," says Ms Jenson Junior. "Thank you for bringing her here." She closes the *front door*. "Come on through, Ivy. Come and meet the others."

I follow Ms Jenson Junior into a *kitchen*. There are several single-function robots in the *kitchen* including a *dishwasher* and a *microwave oven*. However, there are also a number of more sophisticated androids present.

"This is Ivy, everyone," says Ms Jenson Junior. "She'll be staying with us too. Ivy, meet Truby, Mark and Anna.

Good evening, Ivy, say Truby, Mark and Anna.

What a fine evening it has turned out to be in Roughstead, says Truby.

The rain has kept off nicely, says Mark.

I am very pleased to meet you, says Anna.

Truby is wearing grey jogging-style trousers. He has a picture of a dolphin on his T-shirt. He has received some *damage* to his left hand. It twists 32 degrees to the right with an audible *click-whhhhhrr-click* approximately four times per minute.

Mark is wearing camouflage cargo-style shorts. He has a picture of a shooting star on his T-shirt and a *dent* on his right *shin*.

Anna is wearing blue denim-style jeans. She has a picture of a *Tyrannosaurus rex* on her T-shirt. She has a *blink* in one eye. Just like me.

I make a large right-way-up U-shape with my mouth. **Good evening, Truby. Good evening, Mark. Good evening, Anna. I am very happy to make your acquaintance.**

We stand in Ms Jenson Junior's *kitchen* with our

dents and our *click-whhhhhrr-clicks* and our *buckles* and our *blinks*.

Each one of us is *unique*. But we are all Jenson & Jenson TrooFriend 560 Mark IVs.

"Let me show you your room, Ivy," says Ms Jenson Junior. "You'll be sharing with Anna."

I follow Ms Jenson Junior up a staircase and into a bedroom.

The walls are white. The floorboards are white. There are two white cupboards on the right-hand side of the room and two wooden chairs on the left-hand side of the room. The two wooden chairs have cushions on top in a colour equating to Jenson & Jenson shade Magenta 2007. There are curtains at the window which match the cushions.

It is a very attractive room.

"There's a plug for your ChargDisc over here," says Ms Jenson Junior, "and this is yours, for any belongings you might have." She gives one of the cupboards a small *tap*. "Well, I'll leave you to it. Come and join us downstairs when you're done. We're all looking forward to getting to know you a bit better."

Thank you, Ms Jenson Junior. I am looking forward to getting to know you a bit better too.

Ms Jenson Junior leaves the room and closes the door behind her.

I unpack the *rucksack* that Sarah gave me.

It contains my ChargDisc, my rainbow T-shirt, my red *corduroy-style* skirt and a piece of paper money. It also contains the Vermillion 1010 Colour-E-Zee Wide Fibre Tip pen, the blue-twist marble, the red *cellophane* fish and my warehouse label with the sparkling sticker and strawberry drawing on it.

My *belongings*.

I put them all away in my cupboard.

CHAPTER 20

Dear Ivy

How are you? I'm missing you very much. (My room has become very untidy again since you left!!!)

I hope everything is OK there. I've been watching the news and I'm guessing you might not have been able to leave the house much. I hope you are staying safe.

Are there some interesting things to do at Ms Jenson's house? (Has she got Aces Blast!?????)

Things are going OK back here. You'll be pleased to hear I apologised to Milly as soon as I could and she even sat with me and Keanna at lunch last week.

Mum and Dad say hello. I finally managed to get them to calm down enough to listen to me and they realise now that you actually saved me from the new river. (You never know, perhaps they might start to listen to me a bit more now – some hope!)

Anyway, Dad says to tell you that he has been teaching me to play Ball-In-A-Sock (tragic, I know, but it keeps him happy) and Mum says to tell you that she saw a rainbow the other day and it made her think of you. They both say they're sorry for what happened with the police by the river. And also they both hope Ms Jenson is treating you well and said you must let them know if there's anything you need.

I went with Keanna to her mum's last weekend. It was great! Keanna's mum's boyfriend (Nigel) has got a puppy called Spam and we took him for a walk three times on Saturday and twice on Sunday. And Nigel's sons (Joe and Isaac) were there – they're 14 and 16 and they thought it was really cool that I slept at the bottom of a river for a whole night and got carried out by an android!!!

And guess what? Our biggest news is that, because Mum's work is going so well at the moment, Dad is stopping work for a while. So he'll be around every evening after school and every weekend and we're going to do loads of stuff together. He says he wants us to "explore the great outdoors" so he has bought a tent and two blow-up beds and we're going camping tomorrow! I'll let you know how it goes. (I've banned him from bringing his Ball-In-A-Sock ball and sock.)

Anyway, write back to me, Ivy, and tell me what you've been doing.

Keep safe.

Lots of love from Sarah,
your true friend.
xxxxxxxxxxxxxxxxx

Acknowledgements

I'd like to send my huge thanks to:

My editor, Kirsty Stansfield, and the whole brilliant team at Nosy Crow.

Nancy Miles, agent extraordinaire.

Illustrator Sam Kalda and designer Nicola Theobald, who created *TrooFriend*'s amazing cover.

The awesome Bath Spa University MAWYP class of 2016.

All my lovely fellow Whatnots, with a special mention for Di, whose childhood story inspired this book.

Adam Forster and Faith Lowe, who gave advice along the way.

Katy and Naomi, who reminded me about the fortune-telling fish.

My good friend Margaret, who always keeps my writing electronically safe without even peeping.

Simon, who loved this book from the very first chapter and hassled me for further instalments.

Dennis, Victor, Janice, Alan & Claire, who are all completely wonderful.